SQUIRREL TERROR

SQUIRREL TERROR

TERROR

Lilith Saintcrow

SQUIRREL TERROR

Lilith Saintcrow

DEDICATION

For Skyla Dawn Cameron,
without whom none of this would have been possible.

ACKNOWLEDGMENTS, OR, GALLERY OF TERROR

Thanks are due to many--first and foremost to my Readers, who would not let this damn squirrel die. To my writing partner Mel Sterling, and to my Beloved Minion Skyla Dawn Cameron, for keeping me sane. To the ELEW for all sorts of mayhem--let's never stop being bad guys. To you, if you have bought this book. I hope you enjoy it.

Thanks are also due to all those who contributed to the crowdfunding campaign to get SquirrelTerror off the ground. Special thanks to Dave Douds, Karen Feldman, and Amy Stead.

Last but not least, I'd like to especially thank Jonathan Feldman, who is very brave. Braver, certainly, than I might have been in his situation. You did good, kid.

And now, let me thank you all again in the way we both like best: by telling you a story...

HOW THIS HAPPENED

*I*t all started with a squirrel that refused to die.

You're holding a collection of blog posts from September 2010 to December 2011, during which I was recovering from divorce and struggling through deadly depression. My allies: the fact that my kids loved me, a therapist who assured me I was not crazy, two or three close friends, my new addiction to running, and writing as if my life depended on it. My dependents: two little people, three cats, and several houseplants. Arrayed against me: single motherhood (though I'd been basically a single mother for years, the divorce just made it legal instead of me being responsible for more of someone else's debts, but that's another story), crippling anxiety, deep despair, daily panic attacks (I've had them most of my life, but I was beginning to have half a dozen or more a day) and the stress of making a living as basically a freelancer.

I didn't know how the hell I was going to make it through anything. I was drowning, but I wanted to avoid advertising it. Still do. So I wrote instead about writing. The weather. Running. Putting one foot in front of the other.

One day, there was this damn squirrel.

Chronicling the wildlife in my backyard amused me. It seemed to amuse other people too, but I didn't know how much they liked it until my website was hacked and I lost significant chunks of the blogging I'd been doing since 2005. The first thing most people asked after they extended their condolences was "Wait, what about *the squirrels?*"

Months went by, I bought a house for the first time, moved, and every week I'd get at least three emails, either politely asking or outright demanding to know where the squirrel stories had vanished to. When I got to the point of publicly announcing that I couldn't find them, and that digging them off the Wayback Machine was something I didn't have time for, what with a mortgage and kids and dogs and cats to feed, I sort of figured that was the end of it.

I had underestimated, once more, that goddamn squirrel's refusal to lie down and die.

Within a couple hours of making that announcement, I'd had my feet thrown up on and my shoes eaten—courtesy of a bulldog with separation anxiety. Oh, and copies of SquirrelTerror posts landing in my inbox. From CE Murphy and her friend Flynn in Ireland, from Kathleen R. who had printed them out to have something funny to read during her twelve-hour shifts in an ambulance, from a fan whose Internet handle is a stag-god.

We just wanted to help, they said, and from that help, SquirrelTerror posts...well, they resurrected.

Stories can be a rope, pulling you from the abyss. The funny thing is, when you're dragged out of black suicidal bleakness by a story, you have no way of knowing how many other people will touch and twist that rope. The rope itself is neutral. It can be a moment of fleeting amusement or a lifesaving grace.

I don't think the squirrel stories saved any lives, even mine. I do know people liked them, and I laugh helplessly rereading them sometimes, thinking of the things I saw that *didn't* make it onto the page. I do know that people—complete strangers—took time out of their busy days to save them, to keep and reread them, and to offer them to me again when they'd been taken away.

It makes me very happy.

So here they are. I hope you like them. Settle in, get comfortable, and let me tell you some stories about a backyard I used to have, and this crazy goddamn rodent with a crooked tail, bluejay romance, the Forces of Gull, gaslighting, a herding dog, a coyote named Phred, and how I always ended up shoeless and screaming...

SQUiRREL WARS

September 4th, 2010

Those of you on my Twitter feed may (or may not) have been amused by my Ninja!Squirrel reportage. Basically, this all started one morning while on the treadmill, sweating out a five-mile run, I saw a death-defying Terminator ninja[1] squirrel.

I'm not kidding. The little rodent leapt (or was otherwise propelled) off a two-story roof, tumbled through tree branches, hit my back fence, somersaulted in midair, hit the ground, bounced (TWICE! Bounced TWICE, I tell you!) and lay there for a moment, maybe stunned by its own daring.

I was thinking it was a dead squirrel[2] when the little fur-bearing Terminator hopped up on its back legs, twitching its crooked little tail, and glared at me. Of course, I was also (breathlessly) laughing at the time. While running, I might add. Developed a hell of a side stitch, too.

---

[1]Ninja Terminator Trailer http://www.youtube.com/watch?v=-SLsA_Opybw
[2]The Parrot Sketch
http://www.youtube.com/watch?v=npjOSLCR2hE

Ninja!Squirrel glared at me, I repeat, as if I had been the author of his downfall. His beady little eyes were alight with what I can only call hellfire.

Since that moment I have paid closer attention to the squirrels in my backyard. Of course, I can't bloody tell if Ninja!Squirrel is among the ones who gleefully frolic while I run on the treadmill, providing me with distraction and Twitter-food. Those fuzzy little things all look the same to me. Seriously, I can't distinguish one squirrel from another.

Still, things...have grown odd.

Yesterday, as I ran, I began to notice something strange. There appeared to be *two groups* of bushy-tailed Rodentia in my backyard, and they were at what appeared to be war or an extended squirrel dance number[3]. There were leaps, chases, aerial maneuvers, and out-and-out clawings and bitings. The longer I ran, the more interested I became in trying to figure out just what the holy hell was happening—and this was while three bluejays and a crow were playing "chicken" over some scattered bread, while two of my cats watched from the sunroom window and made throaty little *ohpleaseohPLEASE* warbles at me.

Of course, my fancy got the better of me. I began to think up a squirrel Romeo and Juliet.

> *Two clan Rodentias, both alike in infamy[4],*
> *in my fair backyard, where we lay our scene,*
> *From ancient grudge break to new mutiny*
> *where rodent blood makes rodent claws unclean...*

I cast one of the jays as Mercutio, and the crow, of course, as the Prince. I was trying to figure out if one of

---

[3] West Side Story - Prologue
http://www.youtube.com/watch?v=bxoC5Oyf_ss
[4] Romeo and Juliet
http://www.youtube.com/watch?v=YrQqFCJl708

the cats could conceivably be Tybalt or if that was Just Too Much and I would have to have Tybalt be, say, a raccoon? Or something? When my run ended and I hopped off the treadmill for my chin-ups and the rest of my day.

Now comes the creepy part.

Same time this morning, I climbed on the treadmill. About ten minutes in I noticed a growing sense of unease that had nothing to do with how fast I was running or how unhappy my breakfast was with being shaken about so rudely. After fifteen I was perplexed, and after twenty I began to be actively unsettled.

There were robins in the backyard, and the little birds I call chickadees even though I can't tell a chickadee from a condor. The jays were back, shrieking at everything that offended them. A trio from the local crow murder investigated hopefully for some bread, and several of the neighbors' cats wound through on their appointed rounds, all studiously ignoring each other. So far, so good.

No squirrels. Not a single blasted furry little tree-rat to be found. Nada. Zip. Zilch. Zero.

I wonder if Squirrel!Romeo killed his lady love's cousin last night. Or if Ninja!Squirrel has succeeded in enforcing his grip over the clans and is planning an assault on my garage. Or if they are hidden, as only ninjas can hide—I mean, duh, that's why they're *ninjas*—and the pirate squirrels haven't hit the port yet.

I wonder, it would seem, entirely too much. And yet, I am anticipating tomorrow's morning run with breathless excitement.

Further bulletins as events warrant.

SQUIRREL MATRIX

September 16ᵗʰ, 2010

Okay, so I now know why that one day was so quiet.

The squirrels were training their Neo.

Yesterday, again on the treadmill. It was the last five minutes of a five-mile run and, true to form, I had a side stitch and a serious case of wanting to be just about anywhere than where I was. I kept running, because, well, what the hell, it was the last five minutes and I knew I'd feel Victorious and Vindicated and all sorts of other words[5] when I was done.

Then it happened. Well, not *it*, but the precondition for the utterly ridiculous I am about to relate occurred.

I saw a squirrel.

He was a big one, too, crooked-tailed and hellfire-eyed, and he sauntered out into the middle of the yard in a few graceful, authoritative leaps. My earbuds were in, so I couldn't tell if he was chittering. I do know he was scanning my yard like he expected an army to appear at any moment.

---

[5]V for Vendetta – V's Introduction
http://www.youtube.com/watch?v=uW6HbZXI9Y0

No army appeared. However...one of my cats did. The sweet, stupid Tuxedo Kitty, who I adore. Of all three, he's most *my* cat. He thinks he's a hunter, too, and sometimes leaves birds (and when we had the field out back, often mice) on my front step. Of course, he totally ruins the effect by being scared of them once he's killed them—when I pick them up he runs and hides.

So anyway, he was going to get himself a slice of squirrel. What I was thinking was, *You idiot, that could have rabies!*

What came out, since I was running and couldn't get any breath, was a version of "MMMmmmmrph AAAARGHNOOOOOOOO!"

That was when it happened, and I realized this was a Morpheus!Squirrel's savior. (If there is a Morpheus!Squirrel. There's got to be.) This was The One. (This probably makes my cats Agents[6].)

Anyway, the squirrel watched the cat bounding for him, and I could swear there was a moment of kung-fu pose before the cat leapt, all graceful authority, tail held out and claws most probably unsheathed. It was beautiful. It was flat-out gorgeous.

It was, however, doomed.

Neo!Squirrel jumped at the last second, did an amazing flip[7], and I swear to God he kicked my cat in the head[8].

No. Seriously. He kicked my cat in the head[9].
In the head.

---

[6] Matrix Reloaded: Agents Fight Scent
http://www.youtube.com/watch?v=JTb1UPc1zvo
[7] Neo vs Agent Smith
http://www.youtube.com/watch?v=qaLvcM-u4ns
[8] Boot to the Head
http://www.youtube.com/watch?v=9bFfeLY3s64
[9] Boot to the Head
http://www.youtube.com/watch?v=9g1Z3V0QBpg

Tuxedo Kitty landed in a heap, Squirrel!Neo chittered and zoomed away. He leapt five feet up, caught the trunk of the plum tree, and fricking vanished. *Vanished.* I hit the stop button—by this point, all five miles had been achieved and I was having visions of a dead cat to deal with—ripped my earbuds out, almost ran into the sunroom's glass door, and got outside just in time to see Tuxedo Kitty zoom under the fence, tail held low and ears back.

I don't blame him. He was kicked in the head.

I stood there, sweating and cursing, and the phone rang inside the house. For a moment I seriously thought it was Squirrel!Neo calling with a declaration of war.

It was a telemarketer. Thank God. (And this is the only time you'll probably hear me say THAT.)

Tuxedo Kitty seems none the worse for wear, just a bit shaken and embarrassed. He came back in after lunch and spent a long time grooming himself and beating up on the other two cats. (To assure himself of his masculinity, I guess.) It was with no little trepidation that I climbed on the treadmill *this* morning.

Halfway through my run, Squirrel!Neo sauntered out into the yard. He spent a long time pretending to dig, but then he hopped up on one of the patio chairs and eyed me directly for a disconcertingly long time as I ran and tried to ignore him. Beady little eyes, big fluffy crooked tail, and kung fu. Jesus.

I can't wait to see what's next. I just hope that fuzzy little bastard doesn't think I'm after his girlfriend. And I also hope he can't get his paws on any weapons[10]...

---

[10] The Matrix Stockroom
http://www.youtube.com/watch?v=Y70vcs3oV14

OH, SMILEY

September 20th, 2010

Cranky, cold, and nauseated. Yep, it must be Monday.

The only update I have to offer on the ongoing SquirrelTerror is that Squirrel!Neo appears to have won whatever struggle for dominance there was. The backyard is now his territory. Even Tuxedo Kitty and the Siamese from down the street (they observe a studied ignorance of each other that reminds me of some married couples) will not venture into the yard while Neo is hopping about. He came right up to the sunroom door while I was running this morning, put his little paws on the glass, and turned his head sideways, fixing me with one beady little eye.

I'm really hoping he's not going to hack into the house thinking it's the mainframe.

Really, I don't blame the cats. He's a squirrel with kung fu, for Chrissake.

BEASTLY COLD

September 21ˢᵗ, 2010

I have a terrible cold. My largest ambition is going to the grocery store to get DayQuil (I'm not completely out of those little orange capsules of DOOM, thank God), milk, and coffee. (Because I used the last of the coffee this morning OMGBBQLLAMA CRISIS AVERTED...) The common cold is actually rather an interesting little thing, when you consider how long it's been with us, how successful it is, and how ubiquitous too. (This could, of course, be only the fever talking.)

So today is for pottering about and letting the next bit of the story cook. The book broke free last night— that's the point in a work where I can feel it taking its own shape, where the setup has been done and now it's just a matter of seeing where the dominoes fall. It's much more comfortable than the first long slog after the freshness of the idea has worn off *and* the last long slog where it becomes the latest iteration of the Book That Will Not Die Stab It Quick.

Of squirrels, I have only one more thing to report: Squirrel!Neo is the unchallenged master of our yard. Yesterday I was reduced to hysterical laughter as the youngest and silliest of our cats—the one so long and lean and big-eyed we call him Lemur Cat—threw himself at my writing window to get at Squirrel!Neo. (There is still a little noseprint there.) I will swear to my dying day that Squirrel!Neo, calmly hopping about in the yard with his crooked tail flicking unnecessarily but very aesthetically every few bounds, shot Lemur Cat the finger. He didn't even flinch when Lemur Cat hit the window, either. Just flipped him off, as if to say "Bitch, I know *kung fu*[11]."

The funny thing is that Lemur Cat staggered back from the window and across the living room, where he somewhat drunkenly but very viciously attacked the mild-mannered, inoffensive little scratching post I spray with catnip oil every now and again. (Head trauma in felines is fun to watch.)

When he had taught that sorry inanimate object its place, he tore around the room twice, leaping from THE CHAIR[12] to the couch and knocking various things over. Then he calmly sauntered back to my writing window (the window that even now bears a noseprint), hopped up, and settled down on his haunches, staring unblinking at Squirrel!Neo, who was digging around in the lavender under my window like he owned the place and was going to take a nosegay back to the Squirrel!Oracle.

I laughed so hard I coughed and choked. Which produced (or moved around) an incredible amount of phlegm. So I lunged for the tissues, desperate to avoid spraying my laptop with contagion, and almost fell out of my chair. *Almost.* Lemur Cat shot me a filthy look, but I did not fall over. I was actually rather pleased about that, even though that would have made the story much, much funnier. I wasn't sure whether or not to count that as a victory over Squirrel!Neo.

---

[11] Neo vs Morpheus – I Know Kung Fu
http://www.youtube.com/watch?v=EmEPXXJ4sKw
[12]

http://web.archive.org/web/20091225002050/http://www.lilithsain tcrow.com/journal/2008/05/the-chair/

In the end, I think I'd best call it a tie between me and that fuzzy little bastard. But it's Squirrel!Neo 3, cats 0; or cats .5 if I let them claim me not falling and cracking my fool head open.

I can't decide if that makes me the referee or the scorekeeper. Further bulletins as events warrant...

MERCUTIO!JAY, MY HERO

September 23rd, 2010

I really should mow the grass.

I say this because the herbiage is now long enough to give Squirrel!Neo plenty of cover as he goes about his business in my backyard. This grants him, as a Ninja Squirrel, a certain latitude of action. Like the peanut he tried to break my sunroom window with this morning...

...this may require a little explanation, actually.

I was on the treadmill, powering my way through the third of five miles. I call it the break mile, because once I've finished it I might as well finish out the whole bloody hour, right? Since I'm over halfway. It's just one of those little tricks I use to keep myself running. Anyway, I was on the treadmill, with a box of tissues. Because the cold still has me in a grip—well, not quite of iron, perhaps just of lead. Something a bit softer, but still metallic.

It had just begun to rain, and I could see the bread scattered earlier this morning for the bluejays and crows slowly getting sodden. If the birds don't get it, the possums will, and don't talk to me about the possums. I am bribing them in the hopes that they will be allies when the squirrels try to hack my house. (I'm not saying this keeps me up at night, okay? I'm just saying prudence is a virtue.) Remember the bread, all right? Trust me, it's important.

So along comes Squirrel!Neo. He's head-down in the grass, tail twitching as he buries something a few feet from the window directly in front of me. I swear I can see every hair on the fuzzy little bastard's rear. What happened next surprised us both.

I sneezed. I grabbed for a tissue, since it was a wet one. (Between the sweating and the sneezing, it was a very damp morning in there.) Something hit the window.

A peanut.

An actual peanut. I think someone in the neighborhood actually *feeds* these beasts.

That sonofabitch squirrel *threw a peanut at me*. He sat straight up, from the tuft of grass he'd fled to, apparently in terror, after chucking the peanut to save his miserable life.

It startled me, so I swore. Loudly. Squirrel!Neo chittered. At least, I think he did, I had my earbuds in but I saw his little chest and mouth moving. I don't know squirreltongue, but I believe I can translate what he was saying.

"BITCH! I KNOW KUNG FU! FIRST TIME IT'S A PEANUT! NEXT TIME I KICK YOU IN THE HEAD!"

And you know, that actually upset me a little. Because I have done nothing to this squirrel other than laugh at the cats when he shows up. Maybe he thinks I'm laughing at him? I don't know. But the injustice of the situation struck me quite strongly at the moment. So I did what anyone would have done.

I yelled back. (Those among you who are easily offended or have tender ears may wish to quit reading now, while you're ahead.)

"MOTHERFUCKER!" I yelled. "DON'T YOU FUCKING THREATEN ME! WHO GAVE YOU THAT GODDAMN PEANUT?! YOU BREAK MY WINDOW THERE WILL BE *HELL TO PAY!*"

Now, I of course knew that a peanut, even flung by The One, would not break the window. And I didn't give a good-glory-goddamn where he got that peanut from. But when I get to cursing, the most amazing things come out of my mouth, things that have only a tenuous connection to logic. I mean, I wish I could taunt like John Cleese[13], but this is the best I can do, so I commit, you know?

Squirrel!Neo fled to the tenuous purchase of a red wagon the kids left in the middle of the yard. As he did, I caught sight of something amazing falling from the arc of his beautiful jump.

Yes, friends and neighbors. I literally scared the shit out of Squirrel!Neo. He scampered off into the plum tree, probably feeling a few ounces lighter.

By this time I was torn between embarrassment, gratification, the urge to laugh like a hyena, the aching in my legs, the fact that I did not have enough breath for all the multitasking I was doing, and a coughing fit. I think I coughed and swore through the next three minutes, an amazing clot of phlegm working free inside my chest. (I will NOT tell you what happened to the clot. I have *some* couth.)

Another mile and a half passed by, and I had almost recovered when I saw the little fuzzy bastard again. He sauntered out, bold as you please, and started working on the soggy bread. (I told you to remember the bread.)

Well, of course, I watched him. It was a tense détente.

---

[13] French Taunting
http://www.youtube.com/watch?v=9V7zbWNznbs

Squirrel!Neo was so busy stuffing his face, in fact, that he didn't notice the bluejay. (I had originally cast this jay as Mercutio, I suppose that's as good a name as any.) One of a pair who frequents my backyard and scares everyone else at the birdfeeder, this particular jay likes to hang out in the pussywillow tree and roundly curse everyone in sight, or the weather, or what have you. He's also incredibly jealous of bread. He won't eat it if he's already full, but he'll be damned if he'll let anyone take a bit of it. The only exception are the crows, who just sort of laugh at him as he jumps up and down screeching.

Anyway. Mercutio!Jay was unamused by this turn of events. He did not do what he usually does, which is stand up there and yell.

No. Mercutio hopped off the branch, glided down, and proceeded to beat the living hell out of Squirrel!Neo all the way across the yard. Once he was sure he had the fuzzy bastard on the run, he started yelling. Again, I'm no good at bluejaytongue, but I shall endeavor to translate.

"SONOFA*BITCH* THAT'S *MY* GODDAMN BREAD! YOU KNOW KUNG FU? *YOU KNOW KUNG FU?* WELL I'M GODDAMN MERCUTIO, MOTHERFUCKER, AND I'LL WHOMP YOUR FUZZY ASS IN *IAMBIC PENTAMETER!*"

It's a damn good thing I'd just finished my five miles. Because I barely had the wherewithal to hit the stop button. I stood there laughing so hard I cried, blowing my nose twice, coughing and sweating and sneezing. I actually got a vicious side stitch from the whole deal, but here's the best part.

Remember that peanut? The one Neo chucked at me? Well, after he chased the One across the yard, Mercutio!Jay flew back, still swearing at top volume, and picked up the peanut. That forced him to shut up. Still, he eyed me for a few seconds while in front of the window.

Then I swear to God, he *winked* and flew off.
And you know what? He left the bread.

A SQUiRREL'S CLASSiC BLUNDER

September 27ᵗʰ, 2010

Eighty-plus degrees. Terrible humidity. I cannot believe this is September, and it doesn't matter anyway, since the book is eating my head. Sometimes the shift from recalcitrant huge book-thing I have to drag with my teeth to galloping bronco pulling me along in the dust as I frantically try to stay upright is extraordinarily abrupt.

So, I only have a few moments, and I should record this extraordinary thing in the quickly growing annals of SquirrelTerror.

I did mow the lawn this weekend—no, that was *not* the extraordinary thing, jeez, I know I don't do it as much as I should, but I'm busy, all right? (Defensiveness, another symptom of approaching deadline.) ANYWAY. I was waiting to see what Squirrel!Neo would think of this, but ever since I hacked the grass into something resembling a reasonable suburban lawn there was no sight of him.

Until this morning.

The quiet did terrible things to my nerves, so I was almost relieved this morning to see the fuzzy little jerk up in the pussywillow tree, clinging in a fork and surveying the shorn grass. He stayed there so long I almost felt guilty for mowing; I imagined him thinking about the nuts he must have hidden and how the grass probably wouldn't provide a safe cover for them now. I even imagined him bemoaning a natural disaster that had descended on his little patch, stunned by the seeming capriciousness. What does a squirrel know of the weekend and the various exigencies of lawn care?

Yes. I felt *sorry* for the little bugger.

I shouldn't have.

He perched in the pussywillow for a good half hour while I ran, and I was even getting to the point where I imagined him sending me reproachful glances from his beady little rodent eyes as he slid back and forth, checking the sight lines and contingencies. He looked utterly hangdog. I even thought—I am completely serious—that when I was done with five miles maybe I'd go out and scatter some bread for him.

That was when Mercutio!Jay showed up.

He glided in to land on his usual branch, silently— maybe he was uneasy, maybe he was thinking about something else—and with enviable power and authority, as befit the avian master of the backyard.

Squirrel!Neo sprang.

Barely had Mercutio!Jay landed before Squirrel!Neo, the doughty warrior who had lain in wait for so long, hit Mercutio's favorite branch like a ton of bricks. The branch whipped back and forth, Mercutio!Jay was thrown.

But Squirrel!Neo had committed a classic blunder. The first is *never get into a land war in Asia*, and we all know what the second is[14]. Apparently, Squirrel!Neo had this great plan, except he forgot one tiny detail.

Bluejays can fly. Or, more precisely, Neo forgot that jays fly...

...and backyard squirrels, so far, do *not*.

Mercutio!Jay started shrieking and flapping, and I swear I saw a flash of triumph on Squirrel!Neo's fuzzy snout before he realized he was falling. He flurried desperately, and *now* we get to the extraordinary thing.

He scrabbled, sliding down a long thin whippy branch, and he almost made it. I gasped, Mercutio!Jay was still screaming as he settled back on his favorite perch (I think he was yelling "JESUS CHRIST! WHAT THE FUCK, YOU KUNG-FU WISEASS? WHAT IS *WRONG* WITH YOU?"), and Squirrel!Neo clutched desperately...

...and fell. He hit a metal bench set under the fence, then did this *amazing* flip off the bench and landed on the lawn, braced on all fours. His crooked tail switched once, twice, and I could hear the theme music swelling.

Mercutio!Jay hopped from foot to foot. I could swear he was doing the Carlton[15]. His beak moved, and again, I am not up on my bluejaytongue, but I believe he was taunting little Neo.

The closest translation I can offer is: "YEAH! WHO KNOWS KUNG FU NOW, YOU FUZZY-ARSED MORON! WHO KNOWS YOUR KUNG-FU NOW? BWAHAHAHAHAHAHA!"

Squirrel!Neo's lips moved.

I could swear he said "Sonofa*bitch*," before he scampered for the plum tree and disappeared.

This does not bode well.

---

[14]The Princess Bride – Battle of Wits
http://www.youtube.com/watch?v=dzaL8wiSjnM
[15] Carlton Dance http://www.youtube.com/watch?v=jKlxjbhB9HE

TRAINING IS EVERYTHING

October 4ᵗʰ, 2010

I only have a couple minutes today. There's been more SquirrelTerror, so I'll just update you on that. At least, I'll update you on part of it. I just...I don't even know.

Apparently Squirrel!Neo took getting laughed at pretty seriously. After his plan involving Mercutio ignominiously failed, we had a couple days of peace. Then, last week—maybe it was Tuesday, because my fence was still there (more on that later, I promise)—I climbed on the treadmill and was actually relaxing a little bit, thinking that I would have a nice easy run without any shenanigans.

I was wrong.

It didn't take me long to realize Neo was lurking about. Not only that, but there was another squirrel in my yard. The two faced each other in sunlit grass, noses twitching, before Neo leapt on the intruder and a fursplosion[16] occurred. The other squirrel would chitter contemptuously every time Neo was flung back.

I actually thought the newcomer was some punk looking to take over Neo's territory, and of course, I

---

[16] Fursplosion http://www.youtube.com/watch?v=m0JpaiOrRo0

started rooting for Neo. (Better the squirrel demon you know than a new one, right?) But something didn't seem quite right, even when Mercutio!Jay showed up, perching on the fence and eying the proceedings with great interest.

Then something amazing happened.

Squirrel!Neo broke away, and I swear to God the other squirrel yelled, "Good game! Now, lap time! MOVE IT!"

And Squirrel!Neo (I am NOT making this up) headed for the plum tree like his tail was on fire.

He shimmied up the plum tree, foliage shook, and he leapt for the fence. Stuck the landing, barreled past a bemused Mercutio!Jay (who fluttered up to the hedge behind, still cocking his head in a bemused fashion) and jumped up into the pussywillow. He proceeded to perform a two-minute acrobatic routine in the willow, leaves fluttering madly, then he leapt back down to the fence and disappeared into the neighbor's yard. Thirty seconds later he was back, streaking across open space past the other squirrel, who stood motionless.

Neo did this *three times*, acrobatics included. I was tired just watching him. Mercutio watched silently, and the other squirrel just stood there, watching, his tail occasionally twitching. He was a big dude, too. At least a head taller than Neo, which, granted, isn't saying much. They're *squirrels*. Still, he had great posture.

After the third lap, Neo skidded to a stop in the middle of the yard and looked at the bigger squirrel. They stared at each other, and then, I swear, the bigger squirrel nodded. They both broke at the same instant for the juniper hedge and vanished.

Mercutio!Jay coasted across the yard, settled in the feeder in front of my window, and had his breakfast. Every once in a while, he would stop and stare sidelong at the yard, as if trying to figure out what the hell he'd just seen. Once he finished pecking at the birdseed, he stopped, his wings flicking absently.

Then he tilted his head and stared at me, like he was trying to tell me we'd seen something momentous. I pondered this as I ran. It was almost the end of the third mile.

"Holy *shit!*" I yelled, suddenly. "Oh my God!"

Mercutio hopped twice, like he couldn't believe I hadn't seen it earlier.

"Holy shit!" I yelled again, as the mileage clicked over to mile four. "MERCUTIO! THAT WAS FUCKING MORPHEUS[17]! HE'S TRAINING NEO! THAT WAS SQUIRREL KUNG FU TRAINING!"

I swear to God the bluejay rolled his eyes at me. He took off in a flash of blue feathers, and I began to laugh. Within sixty seconds, though, I'd stopped laughing, and not just because I was running.

Because I'd realized, you see, that Neo in training...well.

I'm a little afraid for my bluejay hero.

---

[17] http://en.wikipedia.org/wiki/Morpheus_(The_Matrix)

SQUIRRELS FALLING

October 5th, 2010

The crows tried to warn me as I was walking back from the bus stop. The local murder was up in a fir tree behind the neighbor's house, and they carried on until I called back. I think they knew I didn't quite understand: I was busy planning out my day. Just let it be known they tried to warn me. It isn't their fault.

This was, of course, the day after I witnessed Squirrel!Neo's training. My fence was still intact. (We'll get to the fence in the next post, I promise. Bear with me.) I kind of wondered if anything would happen while I was on the treadmill, but it was dead quiet.

Too quiet.

I did see Mercutio!Jay, stuffing himself with bread in the usual manner. The crows came down and picked at the bread too, ignoring Mercutio's bad-tempered screeching. They paid me no mind, having apparently done all they could. All was serene.

It wasn't until I was on my fifth and final mile that I realized something was happening. I tore my earbuds out and listened, trying to focus over the soughing of my breath and the sound of the treadmill's motor, the pounding of my feet. If I still had the old squeaky treadmill I never would have noticed it. Scrabbling sounds? Something?

What the hell is that? I listened as hard as I could all through the final mile, which passed agonizingly slowly without music. *Huh. It's coming from the roof.*

As soon as I finished the last mile I hit the stop button. Breathing hard, covered in sweat, I cocked my head and was rewarded.

Well, maybe rewarded isn't the right word. It sounded like there was a goddamn moose on my roof.

What the— I seriously did not even get to finish the thought. It was at that moment the squirrel fell.

It gamely tried to grab the birdfeeder hanging in front of the sunroom window, missed, and plunged to the grass. It was up again in an instant, shaking its head, and another one followed, making the same desperate grab for the feeder.

"Jesus!" I yelled, actually flinching. Squirrels 1 and 2 scrambled for the fence to my right, buttonhooking around the edge of my garage, and the scrabbling on the roof intensified.

And another squirrel fell.

I stared. *It's raining Rodentia. No, they've gone lemming. Wait—they're lying in wait for Santa a few months early. What the bloody hell?*

Another squirrel hurtled down, making the same grab for the feeder. "Ohhhhhhh," I breathed. "You sonsabitches! *That's for the bloody birds, you morons!*"

I kept ranting. The squirrels kept falling.

At this point I realized I was standing on my treadmill, dripping with sweat, screaming in my sunroom while squirrels streaked to earth like meteors. I realized there was about five of them, and they were running laps—around the corner of my garage, up the juniper bush around the front, onto the roof, across the house to the sunroom, and searching for a way to get to the birdfeeder. They were determined, and one actually grabbed the lip of the feeder and was spun as it twirled on its rope, then shaken off and flung to the ground. By that point, they were all looking a bit stunned.

The last one to fall off was Squirrel!Neo. I'd recognize that cocked tail and beady glare anywhere. He lay for a second in the dew-wet grass, then hopped to his feet and stared at me. We stood like that, woman and squirrel, both of us out of breath. I swallowed the last half of the sentence I was about to yell.

This isn't over, he seemed to be saying. *Bitch, this is* ***so*** *not over.*

At this point, I'm afraid, my temper snapped. "Oh, yeah?" I put both hands on my hips. "Bring it, you fuzzy-assed moron. *Bring it.*"

As soon as the words were out of my mouth, he scampered away. There was a final scurry on my roof, heading for the bedrooms' roof and the hedge and fence. The squirrels all disappeared into the hedge, and I began to feel a little nervy. I tried to tell myself it was just a squirrel, and after all, I had Mercutio on my side, right? I was the tool-using mammal with the opposable thumb and thousands of years of technology on my side. I could handle a squirrel.

I had no idea what was coming.

NEO AND THE FENCE

October 7th, 2010

And now, about my fence.

A couple days after Squirrel Matrix Training, a day or so after the falling squirrels, I shambled to the treadmill in a fog. I yawned, climbed on, suppressed a coffee-tasting burp...and realized something was not quite right.

There was a huge bloody hole in my fence. I went out to examine, my jaw suspiciously loose.

I have a chain link fence with those plastic strips worked through the links for privacy. The metal bits were still standing, but the plastic was gone in a five-plus-foot hole right behind the plum tree. At first I thought it was some kind of chemical, since the strips were gnarly-melted.

"Sonofa*bitch*," I said, plus other words too.

It used to be a beautiful field back behind my house. Alas, the Powers of Development arose and stuck an apartment complex there. It would be fine if the kids from the complex didn't throw rubbish over my fence, or steal things out of my backyard before I put a lock on the gate—and let's not even talk about the petty vandalism on the padlocks I put in, until the hedge-bushes managed to grow enough to make it hard to get to. The whole thing is compounded by the fact that there's a humongous dustbin right behind said back gate, so there's all sorts of bloody hijinks and interesting smells.

Anyway, there was the hole in my fence and I couldn't do anything about it right at the moment. So I decided to repair to the treadmill and think about things. I didn't trust my temper without exercise to ameliorate it, and the fence was already damaged. I was already in my exercise togs, I might as well get the run out of the way, take a shower, and then start planning. It sounded a very adult thing to do.

Right as my first mile clocked over, I saw the maintenance man from the complex taking pictures of the hole from his side of the fence, wedged into a convenient hole in the hedge. I was off the treadmill in two seconds and in the backyard to meet him.

"I hope you're as concerned about this as I am," was my opening shot.

The poor guy. Apparently there had been a fire the previous afternoon. Someone had called him instead of calling 911, it was a miracle the fire hadn't spread to the plum tree or the juniper. And now here I was, breathing hard like a crazy woman, sweating a little, and in exercise gear.

"Damn kids," I prompted. "This isn't the first time we've had problems."

He sighed, his shoulders slumped. "Well, yeah. I'm going to see if the landscapers can trim the bushes away, so parents can see their kids playing..."

I gave him an *are-you-high?* sort of look. I mean, come on. If the parents were paying attention the little cheeseheads wouldn't be throwing crap over my fence all the time. "Um, that's not such a good idea for me," I said, rather diplomatically I think. "When the bushes were smaller we had a lot more rubbish thrown over the fence."

He winced. "Well, you can just throw it back..." He seemed physically unable to end a sentence with a period. Instead he'd trail off, hang his head to the side a little, and give me a sheepish look.

That's not the **point**, I thought, but manfully restrained myself. I did extract a halfass promise to get my fence fixed, which I will no doubt have to twist an arm or two to have made good upon. I don't even want to think about that right now, it makes me tired. At this point I just wanted to go back and finish my run, and I was pretty sure he wanted to be anywhere else but there talking to me.

Then Maintenance Man glanced up over my shoulder. "Huh."

I looked back. And I flinched.

Squirrel Neo was on the roof. Beady gaze fixed upon us, he chittered loudly. I didn't need a squirreltongue dictionary to figure out it was a war cry.

"Oh no," I said. I was presented with one of those exotic moments—how do you explain to a guy just doing his job that a squirrel knows kung fu? How do you even begin to explain the squirrels falling out of the sky? Where do you even *start* with something like this?

I was saved the trouble. Neo hurled himself across my roof, leapt off, spun on the birdfeeder a couple times, was flung through the air, landed in the middle of my yard, and came scampering straight for us.

I didn't have time to say more than "AUGH!" Maintenance Man let out a "Jesus Christ!" worthy of King Arthur[18]. Imagine two grown adults quailing as a squirrel leaps through ankle-high grass—look, we've

---

[18]Holy Grail – Killer Bunny
http://www.youtube.com/watch?v=XcxKIJTb3Hg

already established I should mow more, all right? Don't judge. Anyway, we cowered.

It was not my finest moment.

However, we weren't Neo's targets. He leapt up into the plum tree and furiously upbraided us. Again, I'm not way up on my squirreltongue, but I think he was saying something like this:

"YEAH! NOW YOU SEE! NOW YOU SEE IT! I KNOW KUNG FU! NEXT TIME IT'S NOT JUST A GRENADE[19], GODDAMN YOU! YOU TELL THAT PONCEY BLUEJAY I'M COMIN' FOR HIM! YEEEEEAAAH!"

"What the *hell*—" Maintenance Man stared in wonder. I was backing up.

Squirrel!Neo scrambled through the branches, extended in a flying leap, and landed on the fence not two feet from Maintenance Man, who let out another strangled sound. Neo scurried along the fence, all the way across my backyard, hopped down into the brush that used to hold the compost pile, and disappeared into my neighbor's yard.

I took stock. We were both still alive. Nobody had been kicked in the head. "Jesus," I breathed.

"Never seen one do *that* before..." Maintenance Man swallowed visibly. "So, yeah. Anyway. Thank goodness the fire didn't spread..."

Did you not just SEE that? I stopped myself just in time. I mean, the situation was bad enough. I wouldn't make it any better by ranting about a squirrel. See, this is the difference between me now and me fifteen-twenty years ago. I know to keep my fool mouth shut sometimes. "Yeah. Thank goodness nobody was hurt. I'd better get

---

[19] The Matrix – Lobby Shootout
http://www.youtube.com/watch?v=_kIGklBRp3s

back to my treadmill. I look forward to having the fence fixed."

And I beat a retreat.

I won't lie. I felt better inside, with the sunroom door firmly closed and bolted.

After that, I didn't see a single squirrel for a couple days. Am I a coward if I admitted I was grateful? My gratitude, however, was short-lived.

Neo wasn't done yet.

BATTLE OF THE PINE BOUGHS

October 13th, 2010

I was just ho-hum, tossing some carbohydrate largess to the avians, when the bombs started falling.

It was early in the morning, after my usual five-mile run, a couple of days after my fence had been bombed. I had a largish store of crusts to crumble for the feathered friends, and I was waiting for the local murder to figure out I was scattering calories for them. They usually sound the alarm, but Mercutio!Jay is always the first and bravest, swooping down after the crows start making their distinctive "OMG FOOD!" calls.

Anyway, there I was, humming a little song, looking forward to going inside and getting a fresh hot cuppa. All of a sudden, there were little plopping sounds.

What the hell?

I looked up. The sounds continued, and I finally realized I was under attack. Pinecones were being hurled from the trees in my neighbor's yard, and an angry chittering broke the morning hush. Not one of the cones hit me, though they came awful close. I stood there with three plastic bread bags in one hand and a fistful of almost-molding potato rolls in the other, staring at the pine trees.

"Neo," I said, out loud, "your aim *sucks*."

I should not have taunted the rodents.

Then Mercutio!Jay arrived, screeching his head off. A flash of blue, feathers flying, he streaked across the yard from the opposite direction. He was utterly heroic. As close as I can figure, he was yelling, "TO ARMS! TO ARMS! FAIR LADY, FEAR NOT! TO ARMS!"

Well, of course, the crows heard his racket, began making a racket of their own, and they swooped in too. That's when things got interesting.

So there I am, sweat still drying on me, in the middle of a ring of breadcrumbs, jaw agape, the pinecone barrage halting as the crows flailed into the pine trees. Mercutio!Jay was in a perfect ecstasy of rage, hopping from foot to foot in the pussywillow tree and screaming "GET IN THERE, FELLOWS! TALLYHO! SPANK THOSE RODENTS!"

I started laughing. I couldn't help myself. The pine trees looked like they were caught in a high wind, thrashing and cawing and chittering issuing from the darkness still caught in their branches. Then the pinecones started up again, and I learned something valuable: they hadn't been trying to hit me.

No, I was just the bait. Because a tiny pinecone hurled out of the tree and smacked Mercutio!Jay, who make a strangled *ulp!* that might have been funny if it hadn't sounded like it hurt. I gasped, he went over in a flurry of feathers, and the next thing I know he'd zoomed past me, flapping furiously, still screaming. "GODDAMMIT WOMAN GET UNDER COVER! IT'S ARTILLERY! MURDER! FIRE! ANARCHY! HALP!"

I stumbled backward, still laughing breathlessly, and I again discovered they weren't aiming at me. Because I tripped over Tuxedo Kitty, who was belly down in the dew-laden grass, watching all this. I hadn't even noticed him creeping out behind me, and I almost went ass-over-teakettle. Tuxedo Kitty squawked as I almost-stepped on him, and he shot off to my left toward the fence. On the way he was peppered with no fewer than three pinecones.

Squirrels are crack shots, apparently. Bombing me had just been to get everyone's attention. I don't know whether to feel grateful or insulted.

So there I was, regaining my balance with a dance step Ginger Rogers might've envied, dropping the rest of the potato rolls and furiously waving the plastic bread bags to signal distress, the ship's going down, someone *do* something, while the pine trees thrashed and the crows made an absolutely unholy noise and the squirrels gave their rallying cries.

Then *he* showed up, winging majestically across the yard in his Capulet blue. It was Romeo!Jay[20], Mercutio's best friend, the strong silent type. (Well, as silent as a bluejay ever gets, but still.) He nipped smartly into the pine trees' recesses, and the tumult reached a fresh pitch.

I was still backing up, trying to look everywhere at once, and Mercutio!Jay circled back to me. He didn't seem to be any the worse for wear, but he harried me across the yard until I was reasonably safe by the sunroom door. Then he wheeled about and zoomed up into the pine trees.

The Battle of the Pine Boughs lasted about ten seconds after that. Abruptly, a battlefield silence fell. I found out I was actually hugging myself, and my tongue was dry because my mouth was open, I was out of breath from helpless laughter, and I was cold. I watched the pine trees nervously. *Nobody is going to BELIEVE this,* I thought. *Seriously. Squirrel artillery. What next?*

The jays appeared first, fluttering down and landing in the middle of the bread. "DUDE," Mercutio was

---

[20] http://movieclips.com/watch/romeo-and-juliet-1968/romeo-kills-tybalt/

saying. "DUDE, DID YOU SEE THAT? DID YOU? YOU WERE ALL, POW, AND BARTHOLOMEW!- CROW WAS ALL LIKE ZAP! THOSE SQUIRRELS, MAN. DID YOU SEE WHAT THEY DID?"

Romeo!Jay shrugged, pecking at the bread. Both of them ignored me.

The crows came down one by one, (Bartholomew the largest was first, as usual) and the usual feeding-scrum developed, with Mercutio yelling at the crows and them laughing at him and eating anyway. I felt for the door handle, slid the French door open, and stepped inside to welcome warmth, backward so I could keep an eye on the yard. There was no sign of poor Tuxedo Kitty, who I had almost flattened. (It was his own damn fault anyway.)

A tiny movement caught my eye as I was bracing the door closed with a dowel. (Just to be sure, you understand.) I straightened, quickly, my back giving a twinge and gooseflesh all over me.

There in the back corner, perched on the fence behind a screen of blackberry leaves, was Squirrel!Neo. His crooked tail was twitching furiously, and his beady little eyes were fixed on the birds. His little mouth moved, and even at that distance and without much knowledge of squirreltongue, I figured out what he was saying with little trouble.

"You bastards," he was mouthing. "You *bastards*. Just you wait."

iNTERSPECiES ELiZABETHAN iNSULTS

November 3rd, 2010

W hat is that huge yellow fiery thing in the sky? It's November, for heaven's sake, we're not supposed to see it! It burns! Augh!

...yeah, the sunlight's making me a little silly today. It's warm and the wind is up, whistling and calling my name as well as pawing through the wind chimes. I did managed to get the lawn mowed, and was bombarded by pinecones. I *think* it was just the wind pulling them off the trees. I'm fairly sure it's not Squirrel!Neo.

He's got other problems.

So I promised I'd write what happened after the Battle of the Pine Boughs. To do that I'm going to have to take you back a week or so, to a gray rainy morning, dawn just coming up—I was on the treadmill early, and not happy about that. By the time I'd gone a couple miles it was light gray instead of pitch black outside, and the little woodland creatures were beginning to show up. Chief among them was Squirrel!Neo, and he had his eye on a lovely little lady bluejay—

Wait. I should tell you about Juliet!Jay. She's a sweet little thing, and both Romeo!Jay and Mercutio!Jay appear to dance attendance on her. She's not a hussy, she rarely shows up with *both* guys. When she does, they seem to want to outdo each other. Mercutio, of course, makes a godawful racket, screeching and "showing" her the bird feeder at least twenty times per visit. Romeo just sidles up and gives her longing looks while they're both pecking at the bread I've scattered. I can't tell who she likes better, although when she does show up with just one of them, it's Romeo. At least, I think it's not Mercutio, because he's not screaming his tiny little head off.

Anyway, okay. So there's Squirrel!Neo, and he's acting kind of strange. Well, stranger than usual. He's hopping once or twice, digging a bit, then looking coyly over his shoulder. After a while, I see a flash in the blueberry bushes—they're turning lovely colors this year, really—and I realize Juliet is perched there, watching him intently. He keeps giving these sneaky little looks, and after a little while, she flies down to investigate.

Now came one of the strangest interspecies dances I've ever seen. Neo would dig a little, glance back at her, and hop away. Juliet would hop shyly up to the location, peck a little bit, and cock her head as if to say, *nothing here, what's wrong with you?*

Each time, Neo stood a little bit closer to her. Then he led her to one of his favorite nut-burying hummocks, and dug. Hopped away, but not nearly as far as before. Juliet sidled, pecked a bit, and came up with something she apparently found very tasty and agreeable. She pecked for a little while, tilting her head back between bites to make everything slide down easy. Neo sidled closer and closer, and I was about to yell or something to warn her, because, well. Who knew what the fuzzy little bastard had planned? I popped my earbuds out and got ready to make a sudden noise, the pounding of my feet on the treadmill all but forgotten as I watched him get closer and closer. I didn't even realize I was sweating, I was so absorbed.

I swear I saw one of Squirrel!Neo's tiny little paws reaching out, as if he wanted to touch. Just the edge of her wing, maybe, some of her pretty plumage.

I think Juliet would've let him, too. But just then, Mercutio showed up, a ball of blue feathered outrage. Since I had my earbuds pulled out, I heard him clear as day in the dawn hush.

"HEY! HEY YOU, FUZZBUCKET! WHAT'RE YOU DOING WITH MAH GIRL, HUH? FETCH ME MY RAPIER, IMMA SPANK SOME SQUIRREL ASS!"

Juliet took wing, Squirrel!Neo scampered up into the plum tree, and Mercutio chased him from there into the juniper hedge, screaming Elizabethan bird-insults. (I swear I heard "mealymouth peasant" and "crude cockerel" in there somewhere.) Then Mercutio spent about ten minutes roaming my backyard, yelling at everything, even perching on the birdfeeder and chewing me out. Maybe I was supposed to be Juliet's duenna or something, I don't know. I don't think I've ever seen a bluejay that angry.

He was pretty incoherent, and Juliet had vanished. I didn't see her for a couple days after that, despite keeping my eyes peeled on the treadmill every single morning.

A couple days later, I found a body in the yard.

SQUIRREL, REVIVIFIED

November 4th, 2010

So there I was. In the rain. Digging a grave.

Okay, okay, let me back up. This was about a week or so ago, the day after Squirrel!Neo and Juliet!Jay had their little interaction and Mercutio!Jay entirely lost his shit. Anyway, for some reason I hadn't had coffee with my oatmeal that morning, I was just going to deal with caffeination after I ran some ungodly number of miles. Just...remember that **the series of events I am about to relate happened while I was completely uncaffeinated**.

So. Kids were off to school, it was raining, I went out to put my freshly-charged iPod on the treadmill before I changed into my running togs. I yawned, glanced out into the backyard...and paused. And stared.

There was a dead squirrel in my backyard. He lay on his back, little paws curled up, soaking in the rain and covered with what looked like mud. I couldn't tell at that distance. I just saw his white chest and his little spattered belly, and he was so, so still.

"Oh, Christ Jesus," I actually breathed. "*Neo?*"

I considered just doing my morning run and then dealing with the, ahem, crime scene. Then I thought of running six miles and staring at a dead rodent, and it just didn't seem appetizing.

I went to fetch a shovel.

This was the straight-edge shovel I bought when we needed to scrape moss off the roof ages ago. It's practically new, and it's a Serious Effing Shovel. Red and black and heavy-reinforced enough to be deadly in the right hands. You could whap someone with this shovel and then use it to dig a grave in rocky soil.

I believe in quality.

There I was, in the rain, near where the compost pile used to be. I was half-soaked by the time I had a decent hole. I didn't want the cats digging him up, or the possums, or anything. The little peanut-flinging cat-kicking bluejay-ambushing bastard was annoying, true. But he had also provided me with priceless amusement and (more importantly) several blog posts. I wanted him buried decently, at least.

I trudged across the wet, ankle-high grass (look, okay, I mowed this past week, all right? Don't look at me like that.). My yard shoes were soaked, my socks were wet, the persistent rain was working its way through my hoodie, and my spectacles were already spattered with rain. But I was determined to Do The Right Thing. I approached the dead rodent with all due reverence, and gently worked the shovel underneath his supine form.

He was heavier than I thought he'd be. *Dead weight*, I thought, and I immediately felt bad, because I snickered. I tried to observe a proper gravitas as I carried him across the yard. My yard shoes are more like clogs, so I was shuffling through very wet grass and squelching a bit, which sort of defeated the gravitas. Still, I tried. I even kept my head up despite the rain smacking my spectacles. I figured a good show was the least I could give, right?

It took some doing to slide him gently into the hole.

I didn't want to just fling him in, all right? I also didn't want him to land all cockeyed and have me out there with the shovel trying to arrange him for his eternal rest. I am many things to many people, but a rodent undertaker is just not in my job description. He was sopping wet and covered with something that looked like mud and dried blood, and his fur was all rucked up already. His tail was a wet draggle. I just, I don't know. I wanted him to be comfy in his little squirrel grave, all right? Don't judge.

I slid him slowly off the shovel bed, and thank God he landed semi-softly. The bottom of the hole was very, very wet—I dig a good grave, thankyouverymuch. I believe in quality work. I took a nice big shovelful of wet, rocky dirt, steeled myself, and sprinkled it in the hole over the poor, wet, draggled little corpse.

I swear to God I heard thunder crackle. The next thing I knew, I was screaming "JESUS CHRIST!"

Because Squirrel!Neo? Had shot up into a crouch. His little black eyes snapped open, and he filled his teensy lungs. He began to produce a sound I can only describe as a squirrel's imitation of Sam Kinison[21] in a blender[22]. It almost drowned out my scream.

This is the point at which I will kindly ask you to remember that I had not even had any coffee that morning.

There I was. In the rain. The squirrel was screaming at me, I was screaming, I stumbled back and lost one of my clogs. My sock squelched in mud, and Squirrel!Neo hopped up to the edge of his grave and KEPT. MAKING. THAT SOUND. He moved quick, too, for a little bugger who had just been singing with the choir

---

[21] http://en.wikipedia.org/wiki/Sam_Kinison
[22] Will It Blend?
http://www.youtube.com/user/blendtec?blend=1&ob=4

eternal[23]. Once he'd gained the lip of his own grave, he actually bounded at me.

His eyes were on fire. His coat was shedding water and mud in rivers. I was out of my mind with fear.

I threw the shovel.

Yes, friends and neighbors, I threw a shovel half as tall as I am at a tiny revivified rodent. But that's not the worst part. Oh, no. Are you ready for the worst?

I missed.

The shovel sailed over Neo's head. It hit the corner between my and my neighbor's fence with a clang that probably woke all the other dead wildlife within a mile radius. I should remind you that the squirrel was still making THAT NOISE and I hadn't run out of air yet, so I was making a high-pitched squeal like a girl in a horror movie.

Hey, I'll admit it. I'm not proud.

I kept backing up, wet sock flopping, spectacles now drenched, and Squirrel!Neo bounded forward twice more. Mud flew. Now, it was a scene of utmost tension, and I'm not sure I heard him right. But I think what he was saying went something like this:

"WHAT THE FUCK ARE YOU DOING? WHAT'S WRONG WITH YOU? WHAT THE HELL? ONE MINUTE I'M JUST MINDING MY OWN DAMN BUSINESS, THEN NEXT—LOOK AT THIS! LOOK AT MY COAT! WHAT THE HELL IS WRONG WITH YOU? BITCH, *I KNOW KUNG FU!*"

At this point I'd run out of "Jesus Christs" and the horror-movie squeal, so I was cussing back. I tripped and went down—on my ass, thank you, and since I've lost a lot of weight it *hurt*, and my teeth clicked together *hard*. Plus my pajamas—oh yeah, did I forget to mention that?

---

[23]The Parrot Sketch
http://www.youtube.com/watch?v=npjOSLCR2hE

I had not even changed out of my sleeping gear—now had mud and grass stain on them. And my spectacles were wet, goddammit.

So I was using Language Unbecoming. Example? Okay, here goes: "MOTHER*FUCKER!* DON'T YOU KUNG FU ME, YOU WERE DEAD! I WAS FUCKING TRYING TO PROVIDE A DECENT MOTHERFUCKING BURIAL, YOU RODENT-ASSED JACKASS!"

Yeah, something like that. Squirrel!Neo bounded forward again. It was like the little bastard didn't even need to breathe, because he was making THAT NOISE again, while he was cussing me out. I yelled something about zombiefuckingoatmealsquirrels, grabbed my other shoe—my only remaining weapon other than my devastating ironic wit—and flung it at him.

This time, my dears, Li'l Lili Oakley didn't miss. I nailed him with my yard shoe. He made an *ulp!* sound that would've been funny if I hadn't immediately felt mortified.

Yes. You read that right. I felt guilty over hitting him with my shoe.

At least it stunned him into silence. He went ass over teakettle, fetched up on the edge of his own grave, stood up, shook himself like a golden retriever coming up out of the water, and dashed to my left. He made it to the juniper hedge and vanished.

Which left me in the rain, on my ass, shoeless, half-blind, calling down the wrath of God onto zombie Frankenstein ninja squirrels and their progeny yea unto the seventh generation. (Who knows? I'm a witch, it might stick.) I finally collected enough of my wits to stand up, shut my fool mouth, collect my shoes, and retreat inside to peel off my muddy clothes, wash my spectacles, and take my morning run. Oh yes, my dears. I ran six miles after that little episode, and I didn't feel a single one of them because of all the adrenaline soaking through my nervous system.

But I sat down and had a cup of coffee first. My hands shook. I kept scanning the backyard nervously, and the rain intensified all that afternoon.

I left the goddamn shovel out there for a couple days, but I couldn't leave it forever. The day I went out to get it, well.

Things got interesting.

BALLAD OF THE HEADLESS SQUIRREL

November 18th, 2010

When we last left our doughty heroine (that would be Yours Truly), she had just encountered a zombie squirrel and left her shovel behind in her haste to achieve shelter. It took a couple days before I was brave enough to go out and fetch the damn shovel, and when I did...things got interesting.

I finished my morning run, took a shower, made sure I was caffeinated, checked the weather—cloudy, but no rain—and armed myself. With what, you might ask? Well, I had to have a hand free to grab the shovel. So it had to fit in one hand, and since I'd had such luck with a shoe during the last run-in, well...I took a Birkenstock sandal. I figured I could swing it by the strap like a flail *or* fling it.

Yes, I spent some time thinking about this. Shut up.

Anyway, I was in a nice warm jacket, my heart beating a little quickly, maybe, but all in all I felt reasonably prepared. I opened my sunroom door and stepped out into the morning...

...and almost onto a headless squirrel.

"JESUS CHRIST!" I screamed, and retreated hastily. The body was tucked up against the door, and I'd been so busy scanning for *live* squirrels I'd overlooked it. I stood there, my heart pounding, and stared through the glass.

Yep. It was a headless squirrel all right. Dead, or at least reasonably dead. Its little paws were pulled up, and since it was splayed on its back I could definitely tell it was a *he*. The edges of its, erm, neck, were all ragged. Something had chewed the head clean off.

After a few seconds, I mastered myself and locked the sunroom door, then went out through the back garage door. First, though, I peered in all directions, and I watched where I stepped. I approached the sorry little headless corpse with all due caution.

Yes, I will admit it. I was afraid it would come back to life.

"Well, *jeeeeeez*," I finally said, staring down. "Guess I'm gonna have to bury this one too."

I edged across the yard, trying to look everywhere at once. This time I had sneakers on, which was a vast improvement. The shovel was wet and jammed up against the fence (I guess I'd really flung it, wow), and the open grave was forlorn, a rain-softened hole. I grabbed the shovel and immediately felt better about the situation. I was all the way across the yard again, looking at the corpse, when I realized I would need both hands to bury him.

This was a pickle. How was I going to keep my weapon while I buried *this* motherfucker?

I ended up looping the strap of the sandal over my wrist, sort of an anti-squirrel quickdraw. I eased the shovel blade under the teensy body with an unsettling sensation of déjà vu, lifted it up, and wondered once again what the hell could have bitten the head off a squirrel.

Just then came a tiny *mew!* I almost jumped out of my skin, because I hadn't noticed the cat in the rosemary bush. The bush is huge, and on the infrequent occasions my cats go outside in the rain they crouch underneath it, in a little bower. This wasn't one of my cats, oh no. My darlings had retreated inside once the rains started. No, this was a tiny fluffy gray thing that usually comes through the yard at about 9:00 a.m. every morning, pausing at a particular clump of lemon balm, then sitting on a bench under the sunroom window for about five minutes before stopping at the rosemary and sauntering away under the fence. She's the late cat—the early cat is a crazed half-Siamese who attacks the fence behind the apartments' dumpster every morning. (I can't make this shit up, I swear.) ANYWAY. Sweet Little Gray Cat cocked her head and mewed again while I struggled to get my heartrate under control.

"You *scared* me!" I finally said, and I swear to God she grinned. She looked very, very proud. "Did you do this?"

She hopped out from under the rosemary, tail held high, and stropped my legs while I stood there with a dead squirrel on a shovel.

"Well, gee." I searched for words. "Thanks. I'm, uh. Just gonna bury him now. Unless you want some, you know, some more."

What the hell else could I say?

Sweet Little Gray followed me across the damp grass. I eased the corpse into the grave and gingerly tossed a shovelful of wet dirt over it, then jumped back. I almost tripped over the cat, who gave me a *WTF, monkey?* look. "Don't look at me like that," I snapped. "You weren't here the last time. I swear to God the last time—"

There was a flicker of motion, a flash of blue, and I choked back another scream. I figure I got another two days' worth of cardio right there. But it was only Juliet!Jay, settling on the fence in the shelter of a tangle of blackberry vines, cocking her head and looking very interested in the proceedings.

"*You* scared the shit out of me, too," I told her grimly, and edged back toward the grave. I got another shovelful of dirt, and I think it was then that Juliet!Jay realized what was in the hole.

She started screaming. I started shoveling furiously. I wanted to get the goddamn thing buried before anything *else* happened. Juliet screeched and fluttered, and she finally took wing, zoomed past me, and disappeared over the house. I heard her screaming for a while, fading into the distance.

I looked at the cat, my jaw suspiciously loose and a fresh load of dirt on my shovel. The cat looked back at me.

I licked dry lips. "What do you suppose that was all about? I mean, this ain't Neo, Neo's got a crooked tail. Besides, if you killed him, I wouldn't bury him. I'd fucking cremate him, you know. He deserves to go to Valhalla, the little fuzzy bastard."

Then I felt bad for standing at the Nameless Squirrel's grave and cussing. I heard something else, too.

A faint, distinct cough.

I looked up. The guy on his apartment balcony stepped back in a hurry, a cloud of cigarette smoke trailing him.

Well, great. What could I say now? He'd seen me talking to a cat and burying a squirrel. There was no explanation I could give anyone for this. I finished filling in the grave, tamped it down as respectfully as I could, and cleared my throat a little. Dude was still up there smoking, I could smell it.

"Well, here lies the nameless, headless squirrel." Maybe I said it a little louder than I had to. Just, well, you know, if I was going to be crazy, I was going to *commit*, you know? There is no point in doing shit like this halfway. "I, uh. I hope he wasn't a zombie. Because you ate his brains. Or whatever made him headless did." I looked down at the gray kitty, who sat with her ears perked far forward, watching this monkey ritual of burying good food with much interest. "May he rest in peace and not come back. And, uh, may his friends not come looking for you. You don't want that, cat. Trust me. Dude's friends know kung fu."

I backed away, stepped down from the railroad ties, and Sweet Little Gray did an honor guard on me all the way back to the garage door. I was still trying to look everywhere at once, shovel in one hand and sandal in the other. I could feel eyes upon me.

Before I went in, I turned and took one last look at the grave. The guy on his balcony smoking was now obscured by the pussywillow tree, and I didn't really want to see him anyway. I let out a breath.

The blackberry bushes behind the fence twitched, and for the thousandth time that morning, I jumped and gave a choked little girly scream.

Squirrel!Neo emerged from the vines, bracing himself on the fence. He looked a lot better than the last time I'd seen him. I shook the sandal, nervously, assuring myself of free play, and then realized I didn't have a free hand to open the door with. Thankfully, I'd left it ajar, so I backed into the garage.

The last thing I saw was Sweet Little Gray sauntering back toward the grave. Squirrel!Neo sat on the fence, watching her approach. You could almost see a tumbleweed skip across the yard between them.

Okay, I'll admit it. I chickened out. I slammed the door, locked it, dropped the shovel, and ran pell-mell for the sunroom and a view of whatever was gonna go down.

By the time I got there, though, they'd both vanished. It took another day before I saw them again. And so far, the headless squirrel has stayed buried...

Well. Mostly.

HEADLESS SQUIRREL, REDUX

November 29th, 2010

S o I was hoping that my third attempt to bury a squirrel would be, so to speak, the charm.

The first time, the squirrel wasn't dead. The second time, it was indisputably dead, being headless. The third time...

Okay. Let me start closer to the beginning. I thought it would be a great idea to scatter the pumpkin seeds from our jack-o'-lanterns over the grave. It *did* occur to me that pumpkin seeds are Squirrel Food, so I had some hazy idea of propitiating the squirrel gods and making an offering to keep the little headless bastard down. (You will notice that I am putting absolutely *nothing* past these fuzzy little ninjas.) Plus I figured it might be good for the bluejays and other little critters as well, since things were getting chilly.

I prepared myself with the Sandal of DOOM and wandered out in broad mid-afternoon daylight, a huge metal IKEA bowl full of pumpkin guts covered with foil propped against my hip. The coast appeared clear.

Halfway across the yard, however, it became clear that things were not well at the gravesite. I'd buried the Headless One pretty deep...but apparently not deep enough. I stood stock-still, caught midstride, as I contemplated the disturbed dirt.

"Well, *fuck*," I breathed, disgusted, and caught sight of the Mad Half-Siamese Cat. This is the early cat that every morning attacks the wooden wall behind the huge dustbin I can see through the burned-out hole in my fence. He—I'm assuming it's a he, I haven't gone close enough to check—flings himself at the wood like it's personally insulted him. After a few body-blows, he jumps up and digs his claws in, gets to the top of the wooden wall, yowls, and then flings himself off into space. The hedge means I can't see where he lands, but I'm sure it's spectacular. *Every morning* he does this.

I don't even know.

Anyway, the Mad Siamese was sauntering along the top of my fence, placing each paw gracefully. He leapt down near one of the blueberry bushes, stalked over to the back corner, and proceeded to flop himself down on the disturbed grave and start rolling in what seemed to be a brand of feline ecstasy.

"What the..." I could not even form words.

He rolled some more, then he jumped up, circled a couple times like he was going to lay down, lifted his haunches in the air, and started digging. Clods of wet dirt flew, and I gathered my wits.

"What the *hell*?" I yelled. "You're DISTURBING THE DEAD, you fucking crazyass feline! What's WRONG with you?"

I must have scared him. Because he leapt—I am not kidding—at least four feet straight up and twisted, landed hard, staring at me with wide, crazed blue eyes. His tail was the size of a raccoon's, and a stripe of fur on his back stood straight up. He actually growled, too. I'm not up on my Mad Siamese, but I am fairly sure it translated out to: "BITCH I WAS HAVING FUN! WHO THE HELL ARE YOU?"

Now, I hadn't gone through burying this squirrel twice to be scared off by an insane, inbred chunk of cat. "Oh, *please*." I shook the sandal in my left fist. "I've faced down a zombie squirrel, a punkass like you is *no* trouble. I'll kick your ass, cat. Leave the dead in peace, willya?"

Mad Siamese took off to my left, yowling, heading for the juniper hedge. I felt good about that for all of about two seconds, because Juliet!Jay appeared out of nowhere, sailing after him with a gleam in her eye and business in every wingflap. I didn't think it was possible for a silent bird to chase an exponentially-bigger cat off, but Juliet was motivated.

Plus, I'm sure my shaking of the sandal had something to do with it.

So I had to get out the shovel once more, because little bits of the Headless Squirrel were sticking up through the dirt. He really looked a bit worse for wear, poor thing, and I got him buried a little deeper and tamped down the dirt pretty hard. Juliet!Jay returned and watched from the fence. She was close enough that I could see every feather, and she examined the proceedings with bright-eyed interest.

"It's not Neo," I finally said, whapping the dirt with the shovel to pack it nice and hard. "Seriously. I've seen that little crooked-tailed bastard running around. You should stick to Romeo!Jay, you know. He's a badass, and he's the strong, silent type. You'll like that. Hell, *I'd* like that. You're lucky. Just consider it, okay? He really likes you."

I just want to register that I was reburying a headless squirrel and giving love advice to a lady bluejay in the middle of the afternoon, while a sandal dangled from my left wrist and a big bowl of pumpkin guts stood off to the side.

You cannot make this shit up. Anyway.

"HEY! HEY GUYS! WHATCHA DOING?" Mercutio!Jay showed up, sailing across the yard and landing on the fence. He immediately started bitching because I wasn't spreading any bread. I swear to God Juliet rolled her eyes. I actually dropped the shovel, the goddamn loudmouth scared me so bad. "SERIOUSLY, WHERE'S THE BREAD? YOU'RE USUALLY SPREADING BREAD. I'M HUNGRY. HEY, THE BIRDFEEDER'S NICE AND ALL, BUT WHERE'S MY BREAD? AND WHAT ARE YOU DOING? WHAT IS THAT IN THE SHINY THING? IS IT BREAD?"

I dumped the pumpkin guts over the grave. "Shut up," I told Mercutio!Jay, who fluttered a bit and didn't screech. "Here lieth the Headless Squirrel, who is *not* Squirrel!Neo. Let's hope he stays buried, because this is really getting—"

"EEEEEEEEEEEEEEEE!" There it was. THAT SOUND[24]. Again.

I let out a girly little half-scream and jumped out of my skin. For lo, Squirrel!Neo had returned.

He barreled along the fence from the plum tree, making that Sam-Kinison[25]-in-a-blender SOUND[26].

"JESUS CHRIST!" Mercutio!Jay yelled. I bent, grabbed the shovel, and started backing up, trying to shake the sandal free just in case. I only succeeded in dumping the wadded-up tinfoil out, because I'd forgotten I was carrying the bowl. I didn't realize I was yelling too. I won't write what I was yelling, I'll just say it was obscene and leave it at that. (I think I used the F-bomb as every

---

[24]The Most Annoying Sound in the World
http://www.youtube.com/watch?v=0cVlTeIATBs
[25] Sam Kinnison http://www.youtube.com/watch?v=DSwG9Tojg9I
[26] The Most Annoying Sound in the World
http://www.youtube.com/watch?v=0cVlTeIATBs

part of speech in the time it took Neo to get to the pussywillow tree.)

Juliet, however, held her ground. She drew herself up, and fire sparked in her little black eyes.

"WHERE THE HELL WERE YOU?" she screamed, and took off for Neo. She hit him good, too, and he actually fell off the fence, through a blueberry bush, and bounced. He quit making THAT SOUND, probably because he was dazed.

I don't blame him.

I was backing up, hopping down from the railroad ties, bowl in one hand, shovel in the other, sandal flapping, my jaw dropping. Juliet, however, was just picking up steam. "I THOUGHT YOU WERE DEAD! I WAS FUCKING MOURNING YOUR FUZZY ASS, WHERE THE HELL WERE YOU?"

Squirrel!Neo, however doughty he may be, was no match for a pissed-off lady jay. He gained his feet and chittered, but she was having none of it. She zoomed down on him in a furious burst of blue feathers, and spanked him all the way back to the juniper hedge. He vanished into the hedge and she spent another few minutes flying back and forth and yelling at the top of her lungs.

"THAT'S RIGHT! THAT'S FUCKING RIGHT, YOU'D **BETTER** HIDE! WHEN I CATCH YOU I'M GOING TO, OOOH YOU DON'T EVEN KNOW WHAT I'M GONNA DO, I WAS **WORRIED** ABOUT YOU! YOU IRRESPONSIBLE LITTLE FUZZY-ARSED MORON! SEE IF I EVER DRINK A POTION FOR YOU EVER AGAIN!"

Mercutio!Jay had settled on the fence again. We both watched her in wonderment.

Finally, she'd finished, coasted back across the yard and settled on the fence, right where she was when the whole thing started. She gave me a baleful glance, and I raised both the shovel and the bowl, trying for a "hey man I'm harmless" stance. She glanced at Mercutio, who actually hopped back nervously.

I cleared my throat. "Yeah. Uh. Okay." I took a couple steps backward. "I'll, just. Yeah. Go in and get some bread for you."

She made a little chittering noise. "SEE THAT YOU DO, MONKEY. JUST SEE THAT YOU DO."

Seriously, would *you* mess with her after all that?

So far the grave has stayed unmolested. All three jays have shown up like clockwork for bread every day, and I think Juliet might be taking my advice. Neo doesn't seem too heartbroken.

He has other problems. Like CornPops.

But more about that later...

BiRDFEEDERS, GANGER SQUiRRELS, AND METAMUCiL

December 1ˢᵗ, 2010

I felt okay until about noon yesterday, when WHOMP! This damn virus descended on me. I'm producing all sorts of phlegm in varied rainbow colors. I'm sure I'm spreading the contagion over everything in my vicinity. I was tired and waspish yesterday, as my writing partner found out. (Sorry about that, kiddo.)

Anyway, there's very little to report. I sent off a short story and am editing Something Sekrit. I do have Very Good News, but I can't announce it until everything's all wrapped. Plus, I still have to write about the squirrels, the gulls, and the CornPops war. I have to wait until I can breathe, because just thinking about it makes me laugh.

I did manage to get out and purchase a "squirrel-proof" birdfeeder. It has a sort of wire cage around the tube holding the seed, and when a squirrel gets on it the cage slides down, barring it from getting any noms.

(Almost like this guy[27], but more decorative.) We'll see how this works out. If all else fails, it should at least be hysterically funny. I kind of dread one of the little rodents getting a paw caught in it or something, though. Because let's face it, these squirrels *would* be the ones to do so. Especially Neo. He's having some bad luck lately.

ANYWAY, while I was purchasing this wondrous object, I also picked up twenty pounds of birdseed. (What? I like to be prepared. It was on SALE.) Then I turned around...and saw it.

SQUIRREL FOOD.

Can you believe that? I'll say it again.

SQUIRREL FOOD.

People *pay money* for this.

I stood there in the Fred Meyer aisle for at least twenty long-ticking seconds, dumbstruck and staring. Three shelves of *squirrel food*. **I cannot believe people feed these fuzzy little cat-kicking ninjas.** There was a wide array, from corncobs to corncob-shaped hanging loaves of seeds and nuts, to sawdust-looking cornmeal things that are probably the Metamucil of the squirrel world. There was *tons* of it.

"No *way*," I finally breathed.

At this point, I have to admit, I did think about buying some of the pressed seed loaves and hanging them up in the plum tree. Why? Aw, just for the lulz, maybe.

No, not for giggles. I'll be honest. Jesus, don't look at me like that.

AS A BRIBE, OKAY? As a kickback to the little fuzzy commandos so they won't break my windows with peanuts or anything. Then I thought, *you know, you start*

---

[27]Woodlink Caged Screen Tube Bird Feeder
http://www.bestnest.com/bestnest/RTProduct.asp?SKU=WDL-WLCMESH

paying the squirrel mafia off and sooner or later they'll start squeezing you for more.

"Oh *hell* no," I muttered. Well, maybe not muttered. Maybe sort of said out loud. "No way. I'm not being held hostage by a bunch of rodents."

I should mention that there was a lady in a red jacket at the other end of the aisle, looking at hummingbird feeders. She gave me a startled look and trundled her cart away maybe a little more quickly than was necessary.

I left the squirrel food where it was, shaking my head. All the way through the store I kept having recurring visions of nattily-dressed squirrel mobsters doing James Cagney[28] sneers. "Eh, here, you see. We don't like dat boid feedah. We like the ones that are real easy-like. But if ya wanna keep that one, sport, all you gotta do is hang up some Metamucil. We prefois it, see?"

...yeah, I amuse myself all the time like this. It's what makes me unfit for a great deal of normal life, I guess.

So. The new feeder is hanging up. The cats are agog, especially sweet dumb Tuxedo!Kitty, who crouches inside on the windowsill and keeps warbling his throaty little "ohpleaseoh*please*" song as the birds discover new munchables. No squirrel has attempted it yet. But I'm waiting. And as I sit here, looking out my window onto my front yard, I can see a couple bushy-tailed ninjas frolicking. They stop jumping around every once in a while to shoot me filthy looks through the window.

I have the Sandal of DOOM right next to me. Let the games begin.

---

[28]James Cagney http://www.youtube.com/watch?v=lqt1kGRsbt0

THE CORN POPS WAR, DAY ONE

December 6th, 2010

Gather close, my children, and let me tell you the tale of the three-day Battle of the Corn Pops, wherein Squirrel!Neo the mighty met his match, a bluejay found romance, and the hordes of Gull were beaten back! Yes, it was a terrible fight that raged from dawn to dusk, and dawn to dusk, and dawn to dusk again, while the mighty-thewed combatants struggled no less with their own exhaustion than with each other.

It all started with a Little Prince and a Fair Princess, and a box of Corn Pops.

I usually buy one box of "fun" cereal and one box of "healthy" cereal. They can eat as much as they want of the fun cereal, but once it's gone the healthy cereal has to be eaten before I'll buy another box of sugar-drenched marketing. I am Best Mum Ever while the fun cereal abounds, but not so much when they have to eat Cheerios or MiniWheats or something. Most of the time I let them come to the store with me and pick the fun cereal. Sometimes I am thrown back on my own resources to find a box of something that fits their exacting standards.

A while ago, I chose Corn Pops. Apparently the Pops were not fun enough. I had a bowl, and they didn't set me on fire. I figured that was because I'm not ten anymore. But the kids evinced no interest in the pure sugar, which is unheard-of. After asking them three or four times if they were ever going to eat the damn Pops, I got the bright idea of dumping them in the backyard where I usually scatter bread for the birds. (Yes, I armed myself with the Sandal of DOOM before doing so. No, nothing worth mentioning happened.)

For two days the Pops sat outside, and I was beginning to think eating a bowl of them had been a bad idea. It's like cockroaches and Twinkies—if the roaches won't even eat that (admittedly very tasty) plastic sponge cake, no way on earth *I'm* gonna. Little did I know that it wasn't the Pops, per se, that made everything so quiet.

It was the gathering of forces, the logistics of warfare, that provided a false lull.

I was washing dishes when I saw the first wave. Four squirrels appeared, converging on the Pops. They started stuffing themselves as fast as they possibly could, and I actually felt good about that. You know how I feel about feeding squirrels, but I was just so glad *someone* would eat the damn things and I wouldn't have to rake up a soggy mess.

I was rinsing my frying pan when the seagulls appeared[29].

They descended, birds of white death. Seriously. Have you ever looked at a seagull compared to a squirrel, even a big fat crooked-tail ninja Terminator squirrel? I mean, I don't know about where you live, gentle Reader, but here we have rubbish dumps, the river, and some seriously hulking seagulls. And they are *nasty*. They're the

---

[29]Wagner – Ride of the Valkyries
http://www.youtube.com/watch?v=V92OBNsQgxU

kind of birds who will knock you down to steal your French fries. (Long story, another day.) They're not as vicious as swans or as smart as geese, but their roaming-in-flocks thing added to their sheer weight means that the four squirrels on the ground were, to put it kindly, obliterated.

The squirrels fled, chittering. Neo was not among them, yet. They scampered away. One tiny gray fluffball did his best to stand his ground, but the seagulls just laughed and pecked at him, flapping their wings until they'd herded him to the juniper hedge.

I am not ashamed to admit I laughed. Loudly, up to my elbows in soapy water. I was not too happy about a sudden influx of gulls—they're all right, I have a soft spot in my heart for omnivorous trash animals, you should see my dating history, but they're *messy*. I stood there laughing so hard I could barely breathe.

Until, that is, the squirrels massed for counterattack.

"AT 'EM, BOYS! SHOW 'EM YOUR KUNG FU! YAH!" Squirrel!Neo led the charge, crooked tail held proudly, swearing like a drill sergeant[30]. I would add "guns blazing" here, except he had no guns. He had only his Matrix training to protect him. It was a glorious charge, him and about five of his fuzzy little brethren. Yes, there were half a dozen squirrels in my yard, and they charged like the Light Brigade[31]. Into the valley of seagull death rode the, um, six or so.

Alas, their heroism came to naught. Or to put it more succinctly, Neo got *spanked*.

I saw one fat white gull laughing as he flapped, harrying poor doomed Squirrel!Neo, the One of

---

[30]Smell of Napalm – Apocalypse Now
http://www.youtube.com/watch?v=6OnOvrTugiA
[31]
http://en.wikipedia.org/wiki/The_Charge_of_the_Light_Brigade_%28poem%29

Rodentia, toward the plum tree. The squirrels would regroup and attack, and the gulls would fence up each time, pecking and flapping, dwarfing their rodent opponents. Juliet!Jay showed up halfway through, and sat on the fence watching with much interest. Mercutio and Romeo, however, stayed in the pussywillow tree, and I'm sure Mercutio!Jay was commenting, though I could barely hear him over the ruckus.

"HEY! HEY DIDJA SEE THAT? FUZZY PUNKS GETTIN' SERVED! YEAH! WHERE'S YOUR KUNG FU NOW, YA STOOPID BUSHTAILED RAT? HUH? WHERE'S YER KUNG-FU NOW? HIT 'IM ON THE HEAD AGAIN, FAT BOY! YEAH!"

I saw Romeo's beak move, too. "DUDE," he remarked, "YOU ARE NOT MAKING THIS ANY EASIER."

Mercutio kept laughing. Juliet was completely silent, transfixed.

Now, my fear of Squirrel!Neo is a healthy fear. I have a great respect for what that little bastard's capable of. But this was...well...

It was *unfair*.

I have this thing for the underdog. Mess with me, fine. I'm a big girl, I can handle it. But pick on someone half your size around me? No way, no day. A sizable proportion of the trouble I've ever gotten into has been me on my nag Rocinante, in my busted-ass tin armor, taking on a giant for the sake of the Little Guy. Besides, I felt kind of guilty. I had, after all, scattered the Fruit of Crunchy Discord in my own backyard. And the gallantry of the squirrels was kind of...moving.

I FELT BAD, ALL RIGHT?

I dropped the plate I was rinsing. I didn't stop to pick up the Sandal of DOOM. No, instead I grabbed one of the Little Prince's foam-wrapped baseball bats.

That kid will never have a Louisville Slugger as long as we live anywhere there's glass to be broken, because if he has a ball a window will sooner or later get the full impact. (THIS is why I only buy wiffle balls.) It's not even his fault, really—I've seen objects *curve* to hit the house when he kicks them. They have it in for him.

Anyway. So I was out the back door, howling like a banshee, waving my bright purple marshal's baton. I was not, at this point, screaming obscenities. Instead, I yelled, "HANG ON, NEO! THE CAVALRY'S COMING! IT'S MY FAULT! JUST HOLD ON!"

I realized I hadn't even put shoes on as soon as I slipped in the wet grass, my socks immediately soaked. I saved myself with an amazing sideways lunge, and I almost punted a seagull. (He was probably one of the rear echelon troops, or a quartermaster. Maybe a cook.) For the record, *this* was the point where I started screaming obscenities. Something like, "OH FOR FUCK'S SAKE, YOU BASTARDS, I'M NOT EVEN WEARING SHOES, IMMA GONNA KILL YOU *ALL!*"

By now, the desired effect was achieved. The seagulls, while they had no trouble dealing with Neo and his plucky bunch of outcasts, did not know what to make of a crazy shoeless woman, spattering dish soap and suds everywhere, waving a kid's baseball bat. They shrieked. Total confusion reigned. The chain of command broke down. The plump white attackers scattered, and they did what every seagull does when frightened: they lightened for takeoff.

Fortunately, I was out of the blast zone. Their parting artillery, however, got most of the squirrels and a liberal portion of my yard. The gulls fled, and I stood there, my sides heaving, still waving the bat. The squirrels were all frozen. A fine misty rain drifted over the battlefield.

Mercutio!Jay hopped up and down on his branch. "JESUS CHRIST, LADY! YOU SCARED ME! WHAT THE HELL ARE YOU DOING? THOSE SQUIRRELS TRIED TO KILL YOU! ARE YOU INSANE?" Juliet bobbed along the fence, free of her stasis. Romeo looked ever-so-faintly disgruntled.

But Squirrel!Neo, showered in seagull poo, looked wearily sidelong at me. I could swear I saw a gleam of defiant respect behind the hellfire in his beady little black eyes. The squirrels limped away, probably to hit the showers, and the jays came gliding down to pick over the battlefield and sample the Crunchy Discord. Feathers and seagull droppings were everywhere. It looked a scene of unspeakable carnage—but at least none of the Flying Brigade had pooped on the Corn Pops.

Or on me.

I beat a hasty retreat inside, changed my socks, and checked the back window frequently. The Corn Pops sat, soaking in the rain. The feathers blew around. The battlefield was empty all through the night.

The next day, the battle took a turn for the bizarre.

THE CORN POPS WAR: THE FINAL BATTLE

December 8th, 2010

*B*eing the final Chronicle of Squirrel!Terror...

The second day of the Corn Pops war dawned just as rainy and cold as the first. I was up before dawn to hit the treadmill, and busy afterward, but I kept checking through my kitchen window. The main bulk of forces were still gathering, I guess, because all day long there was only one gull and one squirrel in the yard at any given time.

It wasn't the same gull or the same squirrel all day. No, as soon as another gull drifted down and landed, the one on guard would take off. Nobody touched the Fruit of Crunchy Discord, which was still scattered glaring-yellow right where I usually dump some torn-up bread for the birds. The feathers had mostly blown away, but the seagull, erm, dooky was still spattered from hell to breakfast all over.

I was beginning to regret buying the goddamn Pops in the first place.

Anyway, the squirrel changing-of-the-guard was a little more complex. It involved a semi-chase and a lot of angry chittering. The exchanges went a little something like this:

"CHRIST DON'T SHOOT! JEEZ! I'M ON GUARD NEXT!"

"THE HELL YOU ARE, I'M HERE UNTIL FOUR!"

"NO, NEO SENT ME. I'M YOUR RELIEF."

"DAMMIT, WHY DOESN'T SOMEONE TELL ME THESE THINGS?"

"LOOK, DON'T BLAME ME. THEY EXPECT YOU BACK AT HEADQUARTERS. HOW IS IT OUT HERE?"

"QUIET. TOO QUIET. HAVE FUN."

Three bluejays observed a scrupulous distance from the Pops. They contented themselves with the birdfeeder, and Romeo!Jay seemed nervous. He kept glancing at whatever seagull was on guard, and would hop a little closer to Juliet. Mercutio!Jay, of course, kept up a running commentary. "WHAT THE HELL? YESTERDAY THEY WERE FIGHTING OVER IT, NOW THEY'RE JUST LOOKING AT IT. STUPID RODENTS AND RODENT-BIRDS. WE SHOULD GO GET SOME OF THOSE YELLOW THINGS. THEN AGAIN, IF SEAGULLS WILL EAT THEM— HEY JULIE, LOOK AT WHAT I CAN DO! LOOK AT THIS!"

You get the idea.

Late in the afternoon, the crows showed up. They evinced no interest in the Pops, they just settled in the plum tree and the pines (the same ones that featured in the Battle of the Pine Boughs) and set up a racket. Finally, the largest, Bartholomew!Crow, coasted in. He hopped around the yard and eyed everything, from the Pops to the gull on duty—a dirty gray bird with a mean glint in his eye—and the squirrel on guard, who hunched nervously near the plum tree and tried to look everywhere at once. He shook his head, cawed a few times, and the crows lifted off.

I was beginning to get a bad feeling about this, but the gulls left at sundown.

The next day, I hit the treadmill before dawn again. I got the kids off to school and came home in the rain. I was halfway home from the bus stop when the crows started setting up a racket. "HEY! HEY LADY! YOU'RE MISSING THE FIGHT!"

I ran for home, tripped through the front door, almost fell into the coat rack, got the door closed and locked, and hurried for the window.

The crows weren't wrong. It was 0815 hours, and the gulls had attacked in force. There was screeching, there was flapping, there were feathers flying. Oddly, none of the gulls were going after the Pops. They just ringed them, the Fruit of Crunchy Discord glowing a little as the sun broke briefly through clouds, and started pecking to determine who was going to get first crack. I stared, wondering if something else would happen—and wondering if I could go and get another cup of coffee to sip while I waited.

I should have grabbed a camera. History would have thanked me, for the third and final battle of the Corn Pops War had begun.

0820 hours: Squirrel counterattack, supported by pinecone artillery from the pines to the north. The Forces of Gull, slightly nonplussed, moved back. They took wing, but thankfully did not crap all over the yard. The Corn Pops just sat there.

0900 hours: Uneasy calm. No sign of gulls or squirrels. Bluejays retreated to western pussywillow tree.

0945 hours: Squirrels moved out in force from southern hedge and western plum tree. The half-dozen from Day One of the War returned, battle-scarred veterans, supported by artillery and reinforcements—two or three younger squirrels. Wiser than the Forces of Gull, the young ones descended on the Fruit of Crunchy Discord and began stuffing their faces *and* hauling it off. They were running it toward the juniper hedge, and Observer had mad thoughts of trying to explain to the neighbors why there were Corn Pops in their yard. Observer decided discretion was the better part of valor, and fetched the Sekrit Weapon. (See following transmissions.)

1013: Forces of Gull counterattacked, scattering the Young Squirrel Logistical Brigade. All hell broke loose. Artillery everywhere. Feathers flying. Bluejays entranced; one male (Codename: MERCUTIO) hopping up and down on pussywillow branches: "OMIGOD! OMIGOD! DO YOU SEE THAT? HIT HIM AGAIN—OH CRAP, THAT'S GONNA LEAVE A MARK! PECK AT HIM, YOU BASTARD, YOU'VE GOT A BEAK, USE IT— JESUS CHRIST, THEY **DO** KNOW KUNG FU! ARE YOU SEEING THIS SHIT? WHERE'S THE MONKEY?! THE MONKEY SHOULD SEE THIS!"

1100: Observer had to leave for climbing. Forces of Gull driven off at great cost; Squirrel Brigade tending to wounded and working frantically to reload ammunition and get the logistical pipeline up again.

1313: Observer returned through heavy rain. Battlefield drenched, soggy feathers and No-Longer-Crunchy Discord scattered instead of in a rough pile. No sign of Forces of Gull. One weary squirrel propped against plum tree, crooked tail drooping, black eyes scanning.

1330: All quiet. Furious rain. Crooked-tail squirrel still watching. Crows in northern pines rustling and watching. Observer took a break for snack and to move Sekrit Weapon to (inside) northern sunroom door.

Civilian chickadees and blackbirds at feeder, nervous but hungry.

1400: Rain tapering off. Battlefield soaked.

1408: Observer pauses while loading dishwasher. Eerie silence.

1411: Observer yells "HOLY CRAP!" Forces of Gull attack in overwhelming force. Battlefield full of feathers, Forces of Gull making ungodly racket. Bluejays in western pussywillow, struck silent (for once) by ferocity of attack. No sign of crooked-tail squirrel on watch.

1413: The **101st Fighting Squirrel Legion (Neo's Fist)** attacks with all available reinforcements. Pinecone artillery firing over open sights. Shouts, screams, chittering. The Champion of Gull crouches over biggest pile of No-Longer-Crunchy Discord, uttering high-pitched squeals.

1414: Challenge is answered by crooked-tail squirrel (codename: NEO), who lets out THAT SOUND and hurls himself into battle.

1414-1418: Crooked-tail squirrel proves he does, indeed, know kung fu. Champion of Gull faintly discomfited. Flying roundhouse kicks. Amazing leaps and bounds. THAT SOUND still being made.

1418-1421: Champion of Gull pulls out his own kung fu. Feathers explode. Champion of Gull seems to have forgotten *he* is flight-capable. 101st and Forces of Gull both draw back, as their champions are dueling. Observer grabs Sekrit Weapon and heads for (outer) sunroom door. *OBSERVER'S NOTE: You see, I'd made up my mind whose side I was on. The squirrels were the underdogs, dammit. And the gulls had crapped all over my yard.*

1421: Observer reaches sunroom door. Rain begins again, after break in clouds and sunshine. Crooked-Tail Squirrel Champion (codename: NEO) receives peck to head that leaves him stunned. Observer yells "OH HELL NO" and tears open sunroom door.

1422: Sunshine again over soaked battlefield. Female jay (codename: JULIET) appears, diving toward Champion of Gull. Squirrel Champion (NEO) lying on Corn Pops, stunned. Observer using language not fit to be repeated. ("THAT'S **MY** GODDAMN SQUIRREL! YOU MOTHERFUCKING SEAGULL, YOU ARE GODDAMN FUCKINGWELL GOING *DOWN*!")

1423: Champion of Gull takes wing briefly, engages JULIET. JULIET is flung back. Silent male bluejay (codename: ROMEO) lets out massive scream. Forces of Gull move in for kill.

1424: Loudmouth male bluejay (codename: MERCUTIO) yells: "JESUS CHRIST ROMEO BUDDY WHAT THE HELL ARE YOU DOING? ATTACK! ATTACK!" Jay ROMEO engages Champion of Gull. Feathers fly.

1424: Help unlooked-for arrives. Crow reinforcements (codename: BARTHOLOMEW and his entire **Legion Corvidae**) descend upon Forces of Gull. JULIET stunned, flutters to her feet. ROMEO kicking living shit out of Champion of Gull. Fire! Flood! DOGS AND CATS LIVING TOGETHER! ANARCHY!

And that, dear friends, is how I ended up outside, brandishing a golf club and screaming imprecations, while Romeo!Jay beat the everliving *hell* out of that big fat white gull. Bartholomew and his Legion made short work of the rest of the Forces of Gull, and the 101st (Neo's Fist) went to town with the artillery. The Forces of Gull decided they'd had enough and lifted off, dumping another load of lightening-for-takeoff, and once again, miraculously, I was not spattered with gull poop.

I believe I have used up a lifetime's supply of luck in *that* regard.

Anyway, in less time than it takes to write it, the Legion had chased the Forces of Gull away. Neo sat up, shaking his little head, and glared around him. The

Champion of Gull was last seen winging furiously away over the apartment complex, screaming in terror. Romeo!Jay returned and coasted down to land near Juliet, who had made it to an azalea near the fence. He pecked at her once or twice, reassuring himself she was all right, and they spent a few minutes in a low-toned conversation that needs no translation. (Juliet: "Why did you do that?" Romeo: "You mean you don't know? I..." Juliet: "Shut up and kiss me.")

Neo hunkered over the Corn Pops, his eyes gleaming madly. My yard looked like a war zone. Or the wreckage of a weekend in Vegas.

Mercutio!Jay hopped up to the scattered Pops and the battlefield champion, sunlight gilding every feather as rain kissed my arms and hair. "JESUS, MAN, YOU REALLY DON'T KNOW WHEN TO QUIT, DO YOU." He bobbed his head. "I CAN TOTES RESPECT THAT. SO WHAT ARE THESE THINGS, ANYWAY?"

Neo, his sides heaving, managed a shrug. "DUNNO," he chittered. "THEY TASTE ALL RIGHT, BUT THEY GIVE ME THE RUNS."

I lowered the golf club. Looked back over my shoulder. A rainbow had appeared, arching in the sky as the clouds covered the sun again and the rain intensified. My spectacles were spotted with drops and my feet were suddenly cold.

I realized, once more, that I'd charged shoeless into the fray. My heart was pounding. Romeo and Juliet took off and settled in the plum tree; as soon as Romeo landed he scooted as close to Julie as he could, and started smoothing her feathers with his beak.

I took a step backward.

Mercutio and Neo both looked at me sideways. Mercutio bobbed his head, grabbed a Corn Pop, and swallowed it. "THESE THINGS ARE NASTY," he

81

commented. "HEY, MONKEY, WHERE'S THE BREAD? YOU USUALLY HAVE BREAD OUT. I COULD USE A SNACK AFTER ALL THAT."

Neo stared for a few moments. Then, deliberately, I swear to you, he nodded. He chittered a little. My squirreltongue could use some work, but I think here's what he said:

"THAT'LL DO, MONKEY. THAT'LL DO."

I retreated in a hurry. Closed the sunroom door, changed my socks, cleaned my spectacles off. At 2:40 (that's 1440 hours, if you're wondering) I made myself a cup of tea and looked out the window.

The crows were back, pecking at the Pops. The Squirrel Logistical Brigade was out in full force too, stuffing themselves and carrying Pops off toward the hedge. Their supervisor, a crooked-tailed champion, oversaw this, stopping every once in a while to pick at the Pops himself. Mercutio!Jay hopped among them, loudly complaining that the monkey hadn't brought out the bread.

And so, lo, peace is restored to the Kingdom of Backyard. For the forces of Bluejay and Squirrel hath reached a tenuous agreement, and the Peacekeeping Forces of Bartholomew Corvidae hath turned the tide of battle. Derring-do hath been accomplished, fair maiden hath been rescued and won, mighty feats of arms hath been performed, and love and brotherhood reign supreme. For Interspecies Harmony hath yea verily been restored, and the annals of Squirrel!Terror now reacheth their end.

...

Unless, of course, some damn thing else *happens...*

FiSH APRiL

April 1st, 2011

It's a Friday and I'm flying low, so...under the cut, the long-awaited picture of Miss B. (ETA: Plus, the Evil League of Evil Writers totally made me cry[32] this morning.)

Hello world, it's Miss B!

[32] http://www.skyladawncameron.com/ELEW/blog/april-interview-lilithsaintcrow

There she is, the newest addition to Casa Saintcrow. This morning she helped me mow the lawn and sat, head cocked, while the yappy terrier next door went absolutely nuts. He was Protecting His Human From The New Canine, and B found this highly amusing. "Dude," she seemed to say, "chillax. The humans are talking." The terrier would have none of that, though, and Miss B grinned at him with great good humor, which infuriated him even more.

I love this dog.

Miss B. has not yet seen a squirrel, although she alerted me to a cat in the neighbor's yard this morning during my run. "Okay," I said, "I see it, settle down." And she did. What a good girl, eh?

BLOODY INTRODUCTIONS

April 4th, 2011

My morning started with a banana and a three-mile run at the low end of my pre-injury pace. This was made easier by the fact that I have finally kicked the flu's ass and sent it howling. Which meant I could breathe, always a plus.

Then it was time to wash the dried blood out of my hair. Now, starting a Monday morning with dry claret spattering one is *de rigeur* for my characters, not so much for me (anymore), so this may require a little explanation.

This came about because I'm tall.

Well, not precisely *tall*. I am a respectable 5'6", though I look MUCH bigger when I'm angry or determined. (This is, incidentally, partly why it's so difficult to buy clothes for me. Or maybe my mouth just makes me seem a lot bigger on a daily basis. Your choice.) This is, however, multiple feet taller than any of the animals in the house. I forgot, while supervising a visit between Miss B and the Tuxedo Kitty[33] (sounds like an indie band, doesn't it) that I would be the tallest thing

---

[33] All names have been altered to protect the innocent, guilty, and just plain unlucky.

around, and hence the safest route of escape for said feline.

Now, Tuxedo Kitty is sweet-stupid, and normally very calm. I am unsure why he's not adjusting to the new addition as well as Cranky Quacker, our oldest cat. (He doesn't miaou. He *quacks*. Seriously.) CQ has found out that if he hisses, Miss B takes notice and backs off. (Her former home had children and cats, I checked before adopting.) So, while Miss B is dying of curiosity about the little furry crankpot, he is controlling the interactions, and doing a handy job of it, too. Tuxedo, though, is hiding with the youngest, and doesn't come out until night or during Miss B's daily walks.

Now, Tuxedo Kitty was never really the same after he got kicked in the head by a squirrel. He seemed to feel the need to prove his masculinity, which led to a lot of Brokeback[34] scenes around the house until Cranky Quacker and Lemur staged an intervention. Two days solid of hissing, batting, chasing, and yowling.

Fun times. Anyway. Afterward, Tuxedo seemed to have something to prove. He's just as sweet and stupid as ever with humans, but new critters get short shrift from him.

So there I was, Tuxedo Kitty coaxed out and made much of, petted and soothed. Miss B was quiet and composed, about four feet away. Then...I don't know. Something exploded. I was on my feet, Tuxedo Kitty got the bright idea that UP was where he wanted to go, and it ended up with me bleeding from the face, head, shoulder...You know, I'm always surprised by just how damn messy head wounds are.

Funny thing about dogs and kids—they'll handle all sorts of things with incredible aplomb as long as the alpha keeps her cool. Miss B, of course, had no clue what had

---

[34] http://en.wikipedia.org/wiki/Brokeback_Mountain

just happened. "HEY, WHAT WAS THAT SOUND? MY BUTT SMELLS FUNNY. IS THAT FOOD? WHERE ARE YOU GOING? IS THERE FOOD THERE?"

Little Prince was slightly less clueless. "Wow. That's a lot of blood. Are you okay? Want me to help? I can help. I know where the BandAids are."

The Princess had her own set of questions. "What happened? Want me to get the cat? He's hiding under the bed. Oh, wow, you're bleeding. Did you know that?"

I think it probably says something that I'm calm even with blood running down my face. Of course, I had two animals to corral, and the kids heard the ruckus and had to be kept copacetic. Once there's bleeding, something clicks inside my head and Disaster Management Lili takes over. Let me tell you, that bitch has brass balls, plus ice water in her veins. So at this point, I was the calmest organism in the room. "You. Sit there. You, back up. You, get in the loo and grab the Bactine. Move."

And lo, they hopped to obey. After a few minutes of Bactine-spraying, Neosporin-smearing (because cat scratches, ZOMG, who knows what those little bastards have on their Scythes of Doom?) and bandaging, I was right as rain. At that point I was more amazed at how high Tuxedo had managed to climb than anything else.

Little bastard was *motivated*.

So that's how I ended up washing dried blood out of my hair this morning. I seriously thought I'd outgrown that sort of thing, but there you go. I'll tell you, it's a lot happier to be doing it after cat scratches than after a barfight. But that's (say it with me) another blog post.

Tune in tomorrow, incidentally, for the tale of Miss B meeting her first squirrel! *evil twinkle*

NEO AND MISS B

April 6th, 2011

Got the end of a kidnap attempt, a messy bloody death, a visit to Wilde the Sorcerer, and the tracing of a shipment of Prussian capacitors to write. This morning was interval training and a multiple-mile walk with Miss B. I think I tired her out. The only drawback is that I can't nap like she does. I have a story to tell you first.

Yes, Miss B met Neo the other day. As luck would have it, this was the first Squirrel-and-B interaction I had the pleasure of witnessing, and it just *had* to be the Terminator ninja death squirrel.

Picture this: a cloudy day, Miss B snoot-deep in backyard grass, Yours Truly leaning against the sunroom wall watching, yawning and holding an afternoon cuppa. It's a tranquil scene.

From the clouds of blossoms on the plum tree, Neo sallied forth, crooked tail held high. Nobody had informed him of the Glorious Advent[35].

"Oh, Christ on a cracker NO—" The last thing I wanted was my dog kicked in the head. That would get things off on the wrong foot. Plus, Tuxedo Kitty was

---

[35] http://www.lilithsaintcrow.com/journal/2011/03/the-glorious-advent-approacheth/

never the same after his head trauma. I started forward, tea sloshing, Miss B turned to see what I was looking at...

...and froze, ears perked so far they almost started from her head, one paw lifted, barely even breathing.

How Neo missed an exponentially-bigger animal covered in russet fur staring at him as her haunches slowly sank in preparation, I'll never know. He sauntered away from the tree, chittering a little as he encountered a small pile of grass clippings. Maybe he thought it was a fine place to bury a spring nut or two. Maybe he was so used to the calm in the backyard he literally didn't notice. Maybe he was simply overconfident.

The preparation only took a few seconds, but it was long stretched-out nightmare time for me. You know those dreams where you're running, but everything's made of lead and you just can't move fast enough? Yeah. Like that.

Still deadly silent, Miss B bolted.

"Watch out!" I yelled, hot tea slopping in my cup. "HE KICKS PEOPLE IN THE HEAD!"

Now, I was prepared for a short sharp flurry and a howling Miss B. She's up on her rabies shots, though—it had been less than a week since her last jab.

I fully admit I underestimated my dog.

"HEEEEERD IT!" she bellowed in midstride, and was across the yard in an eye-blink.

"WHAT TH—EEEEEEEEE!" Neo started Making That Sound again. He bolted for the plum tree, but Miss B cut him off.

I watched my new Aussie herd the Terminator death ninja squirrel across my yard, harrying and nipping, turning on a dime, anticipating, and generally treating him like a flock of sheep. Now, squirrels are generally very nimble little critters, and Neo doubly so. But Miss B had her nose down, and she cut him off every. Single. Time. Grass flew. Neo stopped making That Noise. I suppose he thought he was running for his life and needed the oxygen. Back and forth they went—Miss B got him turned around near the fence, he feinted, she took the bait, he reversed—but so did she, with sweet natural grace, nipping at his crooked tail for good measure.

I stood there, mouth ajar, tea pouring out of my dangling cup. It was actually the boiling-hot tea splashing through my pants that restored me to some kind of sanity. "B——!" I used her full name and my You Are My Child voice. She skidded to a stop, head up, eying me.

Neo darted for the shelter of the plum tree. Miss B quivered with anticipation. "No," I said, "let the fuzzy little bastard rest. You've had your fun."

She chuffed and trotted back to me, head high, her hindquarters wriggling with delight. "I HERDED IT! IT WAS A QUICK LITTLE BASTARD TOO! DID YOU SEE ME HERD IT? IS THAT MY NEW JOB?"

"Just be careful," I told her, snorting for breath through the laughter. "That's no ordinary squirrel. Plus he's probably going to bring backup."

Blossom-laden branches shook violently. Squirrel!Neo was invisible, but I could certainly hear him. "WHAT THE...WHAT WAS THAT? WHAT IS THAT? THE MONKEY'S TALKING TO IT! THERE'S SOMETHING IN THE YARD! FIRE! FLOOD! ANARCHY! **IT NEARLY GOT ME**!"

That did me in. I leaned against the house and fair wheezed with laughter. My stomach hurt and I had to blow my nose by the time I was done. Miss B, of course, kept one eye on me and one eye on the plum tree, waiting for Round Two.

This is gonna be good.

iNTRODUCiNG STEERPiKE SQUiRREL

May 4ᵗʰ, 2011

It's a bright sunny day. Which means two things: spring is here, and after I take the kids to the dentist (boo!) I can take them to the park (yay!). The Princess is excited about staying home from school and sleeping in, while the Prince is downcast because he will miss his friends. I am cautiously waiting to see if the mercury will reach 70F today, which will be a cause for celebration—or, more likely, just a mowing of the lawns. For lo, the herbiage around my humble abode doth need a clipping. If only to make the approaches more visible so the squirrels can't sneak up.

Though really, I think the squirrels have decided Miss B is too much trouble, since there is internal strife in Squirrelandia. Yes, Neo's throne...is in danger.

Now, Squirrel!Neo's leadership was much in evidence during the Corn Pops War, and all through the wet, mostly-warmish winter we had. Despite that, there must have been grumbles of discontent—war heroes can't live on their laurels forever. The little rodents were pretty active this winter, because the temperatures didn't plunge nearly as much as they have in winters past, but the fact that it was, well, you know, *winter* meant that there wasn't much in the way of calories to fuel that activity. The proportion of idiots in my neighborhood who actually feed the blasted animals seems to be constant, but there still wasn't enough food to go round.

Squirrel!Neo savaged local birdfeeders, ravaged bulb plantings, and led his people all through the dismal winter, but now it's spring and there's a fresh crop of young squirrels looking to get a piece of the alpha squirrel action. Or something. Chief among them is a wiry reddish-coated lad I've named Steerpike[36]!Squirrel, for his habit of pawing his way delicately along my back fence as if he's tip-tapping over Gormenghast roofs. He moves with much deliberation, this kitchen-boy-turned-wannabe-squirrel-dictator.

Anyway, this little guy has pounced on Neo and gotten smacked down more than once. Neo looks unconcerned—or, you know, as Ruler of Squirrelandia he has bigger problems. Steerpike!Squirrel doesn't seem to be a Brutus[37], since he and Neo aren't friends—he's more a Cassius[38], a lean and hungry type.

Such squirrels are dangerous.

Miss B doesn't like Steerpike!Squirrel either. Instead of the way she watches Neo—ears perked, body tense, grinning happily, just aching for him to come down and play so she can HEEEEERD him—with Steerpike, she narrows her eyes and sits, never turning her back to him. And should he be in the yard when she goes out to do her business there is no HEEEEERD-ing. There is a low snaking motion of her head, and she bolts right for him, teeth bared.

---

[36] http://en.wikipedia.org/wiki/Steerpike

[37] http://en.wikipedia.org/wiki/Marcus_Junius_Brutus_the_Younger

[38] http://en.wikipedia.org/wiki/Gaius_Cassius_Longinus

I think she sees Neo as a playmate, and Steerpike as potential food. Or, you know, vermin.

Anyway, Squirrelandia is feeling the tension these days. The food situation has eased up, but the rodents are still restless. Whenever Neo appears, doing his squirrel-business, I can usually look and find Steerpike in some shadowed corner. Watching. Waiting.

This does not bode well.

JORPEL BUNNIES, MISS B, AND PHRED

September 1st, 2011

The kids are back in school. Which means I'm getting up at 5:00 a.m. again, but instead of running on the treadmill, I've taken to running outside.

In the dark. With the dog. Which is pretty much how you'd think it would be. If I could fit the dog on the treadmill for my long runs I would, but on that path lies madness. Best just to get out the door, take my lumps, and haul ass through rain and whatnot.

Predawn. Mist rising off the athletic fields at the middle and elementary schools. Miss B trots along beside me, unsure just what we're doing at this godforsaken hour, but she's got her backpack on and it's obviously time to work, so she's down for it. (There's none of this "I don't want to get up" bullshit from Miss B, oh no. The instant I stir in the morning it's a cold wet nose to the face and a "SOHAPPYTOSEEYOU, MISSEDYOU SOMUCH, WHATWEDOINGNOW?")

Nobody out except us and a few people driving to work, and the morning bicycle-riders. (CRAZY. You couldn't *pay* me to do that. To each their own insanity, though, right?) The only sounds are my breathing, the jingle of Miss B's collar, the pounding of my feet. The usual dogs on our route don't know what to make of us this early; it will take time for them to realize we're just out running and they can relax.

So, it's fairly tranquil. Except for (you knew there had to be an "except for", didn't you?) the killer bunnies[39].

You see, someone's pet rabbits escaped. As rabbits will do, they went feral and started breeding. They're not a neighborhood plague—not quite, not yet. But they're fluffy and cottontailed, and very fast.

Miss B would looooove to catch herself some rabbit. Mind you, she probably wouldn't have the faintest idea what to do if she *actually did get one*. It's one of the Great Unfulfilled Desires of her life, kind of like Catching An SUV or Fitting Underneath The Alpha's Bed, or even Getting Her Nose Up The UPS Guy's Bottom. She's a herding dog, so she sees something bolt and every circuit in her head fuses. She takes off, dead silent, and the only thing stopping her is the leash tied around my waist. Now, she's forty-plus pounds of dog, more all the time since she eats well, and I'm *mumblemumble* pounds of human, so those are fun times. Let's just say that the leash is slip-knotted for a reason, and that I know how to drop my center of gravity and keep going.

Yet *another* lesson I am very grateful to belly dancing for.

Anyway, when I had the bright idea of running outside before dawn, I hadn't thought about the fact that right before sunup is when the little vorpel bunnies were going to be out and active. So half of our morning run takes place around an elementary school playing field that

---

[39] Holy Grail – Killer Bunny
http://www.youtube.com/watch?v=XcxKIJTb3Hg

is, coincidentally, Grand Bunny Central. It's like an obstacle course, and also sharpens my night vision. I can tell I'm about to become very adept at bracing myself right before Miss B lunges after Peter Cottontail, who pauses to give her the finger before laughing, sticking his bum in the air, and taking off at warp fifteen.

This morning we hit Grand Bunny Central, we're about a mile and a half in, things are warmed up and going nicely. Miss B starts acting a little funny. I can't quite tell what she's getting the scent of, but apparently it is FANTASTIC. If her tail wasn't naturally docked, it would be wagging itself right off her rump. In any event, she's trying to wag so hard her back end is skipping around, which usually means she's seen another dog and wants to make friends. I don't know how she can run an 11.5-minute mile while her back end is doing the Funky Chicken, but some mysteries are not meant for mortals to solve.

There's a tawny-gray flash out of the corner of my eye, there and gone. Miss B is almost hysterical with joy. Something is in the neighborhood, running roughly parallel to us. It veers away through a passage between two houses, and I forget about it. Maybe a stray, maybe a cat, who knows? It was too big to be a bunny, that's all I could tell.

We make the hard left turn into the park near the elementary school, and Miss B is unwontedly eager. Still, we haven't hit the three-mile mark, which is when she usually calms down. So we're going along, and all of a sudden there's that tawny-gray flash again. Four legs, running low. It stops, ears perked high, and Miss B pleads to be allowed to go make friends.

ME: Huh, that's odd. It's canine...pretty small to be shaped like that, though, wonder what breed—

MISS B: NEW FRIEND! NEW FRIEND! NEWFRIEND NEWFRIENDNEWFRIEND!

ME: And that's a strange color, too—HOLY SHIT GET IN THE CAR[40] IT'S A COYOTE!

MISS B: CAN WE PLAY NEW FRIEND NEW FRIEND, OH PLEASE OH PLEASE—

ME: NO IT PROLLY HAS RABIES JESUS STOP IT LET'S GET OUT OF HERE!

PHRED THE COYOTE: Chillax, you guys are scaring the rabbits!

Yep, you read that right. A coyote. In the middle of the neighborhood. He probably comes down from the hills to hunt wabbit[41]. I don't know if Miss B has ever seen a coyote before. She certainly wanted to make Phred's acquaintance, in a big, big way. No barking, but that back of the throat *ohcomeon* whine she uses when she just wants to play with another dog. And me, grimly running onward—Miss B and I, we could probably take anything short of a pack of hyenas, but she is looking like she'd be no help. Plus, if Phred is going to put a dent in the rabbit population, he's welcome to go about his business.

See, I love crows and coyotes and seagulls. I love the omnivorous trash animals, the ones that creep around the corner and do Nature's dirty cleanup work. They're usually smart as hell and interesting to boot. So as long as Phred keeps to his bidness, we'll keep to ours.

He just better not come a few streets over and start messing with cats instead of bunnies. Because then, shit will get real. I will sic Neo on him.

Speaking of Neo...but that's tomorrow's story.

See you then!

---

[40] "Jesus Christ, it's a lion! Get back in the car!"
http://cheezburger.com/4362518016
[41] Kill the Wabbit
http://www.youtube.com/watch?v=Yxiv3CBMS4M

TROUBLE IN THE LAND OF BACKYARD

September 2nd, 2011

Predawn. The world is hushed and gray. A rabbit goes streaking across the field, but Miss B takes no notice. Her ears are perked, she is expectant—

—and Phred the Coyote, low to the ground and moving deadly-fast, grabs the bunny neat as you please. A snap and a shake, Mr. Lapin didn't even have time to scream.

Phred looked up with a mouthful of fur as we passed. I swear to God he said, "MRPHLE!" Which is, I guess, coyote-talk for "Ohai! Gotta go. Breakfast." He trotted off, vanishing into underbrush near a fence. Miss B kept looking up at me.

Seriously? she was saying. *Really? Is that what you do when you catch one? REALLY?*

I sense trouble in our future.

Anyway. Today I want to take you back a few months. There was trouble in the land of Backyard, but it started very small.

WHEN LAST WE SAW Squirrel!Neo, he was the victorious general of the Corn Pops War. He was Big Man on Campus. He swaggered. He had all the babes. But there was another squirrel in the wings, a little reddish thing with a gleam in his nasty rodent eyes. He was lean and hungry, and such squirrels are dangerous[42].

It was subtle, at first. Steerpike!Squirrel (for so he was named, this lean hungry one) was in the background, watching as Neo swaggered. Then he moved forward, and for a while, there were no better friends than the victorious general and the whip-thin youngster. There were babes aplenty (and apparently it was mating season, DO NOT ASK FOR THAT STORY, just trust me) and Steerpike!Squirrel was always on hand to fetch and carry.

Still, there was one disturbing incident.

Your humble narrator was washing dishes one fine, partly-sunny afternoon (it does happen) and gazing reflectively out the kitchen window. Squirrel!Neo pranced past, alone for once, a lone gray squirrel with a crooked tail, veteran of many wars, the very Squirrel Revivified. He lashed that crooked tail, paused to admire the bank of fragrant rosemary swarming with busy bees...

...and a pinecone smacked right into his head.

Neo tumbled, his warrior reflexes a little rusty but still good. Two more pinecones plowed into the ground around him as he rolled. "ARTILLERY!" he yelled. "GET DOWN GET DOWN, WHERE'S THE GODDAMN PLATOON, GET THE TANK KILLER BRIGADE!"

I stopped, holding a pasta pot that needed scrubbing, and stared openmouthed. Squirrel!Neo kept rolling, got his feet underneath him, and scrabbled for the fence. He vanished into the juniper hedge, and I cocked my head. "Huh."

---

[42] http://www.online-literature.com/shakespeare/julius_caesar/3/

A few moments later, as I was rinsing the gleaming pasta pot, who should appear but Steerpike!Squirrel, slithering from the pine trees and cutting across the corner of the yard. He moved low and slow, glancing around to make certain he wasn't being witnessed.

"Huh," I repeated, and even though I was inside the house, perhaps he heard me. He halted and glanced over his shoulder, staring at the kitchen window with disconcerting directness. A flash of crimson far back in his pupils, and he was up the fence in a moment, and gone.

I suspected worse was to come.

I was right.

THE GASLIGHTING OF NEO

September 6th, 2011

Another predawn sighting of Phred the Coyote. The Bunny Brigade was taunting him, but they lost another one of their number. Ah, the circle of life. Miss B has figured out that she wants nothing to do with him, but he'd be so *fun* to *heeeeerd*. Apparently I'm Mean and Cruel and Unjust for insisting that she do no such thing.

Anyway, when last we spoke, I was telling you about the mysterious peppering of Squirrel!Neo with pinecones. I saw Steerpike!Squirrel slinking away afterward, but that wasn't, so to speak, proof enough to convict. It was, however, enough to make me wonder and keep an eye out.

Picture this: a cloudy afternoon, the squirrels going about their business. You know how, in a group of people, a sudden silence will fall? (*Hermes is among us*, they used to say.) It's kind of like that in the Kingdom of Backyard. There will be a crowd, and all of a sudden, everyone will disappear except for one lone squirrel. He's got a crooked tail, and he's a little bigger than Yon

Average Yard Rodent. He glances around, sees that he is alone, and immediately is on high alert.

Because that's when it strikes. A pinecone, a small rock, any type of ammunition. Always when he was alone, always from an unexpected direction. Other squirrels would show up and give him curious looks as he stood, shaking his fist and chittering angrily, or desperately trying to convince them to stay under cover.

The first stage was anger, of course. He'd be pelted, and would take out his aggression on the first thing he saw. Most of the time it was other squirrels. But this particular afternoon, he was bombed from the plum tree with something that looked suspiciously like an acorn. (I don't know where the hell it came from, there's not an oak tree for a few *miles*.) Neo hit the dirt, rolling, and just barely avoided getting hit in the head. He came up, furious and looking for the perpetrator...

...just as Romeo!Jay, his brother-in-arms, glided down to land near him and shoot the breeze. Romeo doesn't talk much—he saves most of his words for Juliet!Jay, as we saw during the Corn Pops War. But he does like to hop around after Neo and his cadre, occasionally getting in a screechy joke that will make all of them laugh. I get the idea that with Mercutio!Jay around, Romeo doesn't often get a word in edgewise, so he's learned to make them count.

Neo went off.

"BANZAI!" he yelled in squirrelese. "MOTHER-FUCKER I'VE GOT YOU NOW! BOMB ME WITH NUTS, WILL YOU?"

"JESUS CHRIST!" Romeo!Jay screamed, taking off in an explosion of feathers. "WHAT THE HELL, YOU FURRY DUMBASS?"

Your Humble Narrator stood in the sunroom with a watering can—yes, I was watering my goddamn bonsai, that's a whole 'nother story—and a slack jaw, observing this.

All Squirrel!Neo's considerable fury and frustration had boiled over. He leapt after Romeo!Jay, screaming like a banshee. Yes, he was making THAT SOUND, like a wineglass, Sam Kinison, and some steak caught in a possessed blender[43]. Romeo, normally an easygoing guy (he used to be a little more wound up before Juliet noticed his existence, now he's pretty damn calm for a jay), spread his wings, let out a warning screech, and pecked Neo.

On the head.

It was a perfect kung-fu peck (where the hell do all these animals learn their goddamn martial arts, I'd like to know), and it rang Neo's chimes pretty good. Romeo hopped back. "WHAT THE HELL?" he squawked again. "HAVE YOU LOST YOUR TINY LITTLE MIND, DUMBASS? WHAT'S WRONG WITH YOU?"

Neo lay stunned on the grass for a moment before hopping up. "YOU FEATHERED BASTARD!" he screamed. "OH YOU FEATHERED FUCKING BASTARD, I'M GONNA—"

"YOU'RE GONNA WHAT?" Romeo cocked his head. "ANYTIME YOU THINK YOU'RE BLUEJAY ENOUGH FOR THE JOB, FOURLEGS. BRING IT."

With that, he spread his wings again and took off, brushing over Neo's head. The King of Backyard ducked as the jay buzzed him, and Romeo was gone over the house in a flash of blue feathers. The King shook his tiny little rodent fists and bayed furiously at the cloudy sky.

That's when the other acorn pasted him right on the noggin as well. This one came from the plum tree too.

Behind Neo.

---

[43]Will It Blend?
http://www.youtube.com/user/blendtec?blend=1&ob=4

"Holy shit," I breathed, looking down at Miss B. She cocked her head, wondering what in the yard was holding my attention so much. "Somebody's gaslighting[44] Neo."

I got the canine equivalent of a shrug—she can't see out into that part of the yard when she's under the picnic table in the sunroom. (Don't ask.) I looked up just in time to see Neo's tail disappearing into the juniper hedge next to the plum tree as yet another acorn-shaped thing plowed into the ground behind him.

I waited.

Sure enough, after an interval, who should come sneaking down the plum tree but a certain reddish squirrel?

"You bastard," I muttered. "Oh, I don't like you."

Steerpike!Squirrel glanced at the house as if he'd heard me. He flicked his lean reddish tail twice, smoothed the fur on his tiny head, and I could swear to God he smiled before vanishing into the hedge after the sorely-tried King of Backyard.

I had a sinking feeling things were about to get ugly.

---

[44] http://en.wikipedia.org/wiki/Gaslighting

SQUIRREL!TERROR MELEE EDITION

September 19th, 2011

How was your weekend? I rearranged my dining room and went to a bouldering clinic at the Circuit[45]. Incidentally, if you ever get a chance to take a clinic with Alex Johnson[46], do. She's utterly delightful.

I've been putting off telling you what happened next in the Kingdom of Backyard, haven't I. Well, that won't make it any better. *sigh*

So. When last you saw Squirrel!Neo, he was being peppered with pinecones and various other materials. (I did not know squirrels could fling poo like monkeys. Well, lesson learned, but I'm not telling THAT story. I have *some* pride. Anyway.)

First, King Neo got mad. Then...he got paranoid.

You see, the bombardment only happened when he was alone, and only in the backyard. When the posse was with him, Neo was safe...but he was also nervous. Paranoia made him mean.

---

[45] http://www.thecircuitgym.com
[46] http://www.dpmclimbing.com/articles/view/alex-johnson-pro-climber

You can't keep your position as King of the Backyard for very long if you start randomly screaming "BITCHIKNOWKUNGFU!" and jumping on whoever happens to be closest to you at the time. I mean, you can *for a while*—but that sort of behavior leads to rebellion sooner or later. (This is the reason dictatorships inevitably crumble. Trufax.)

And what, you may ask, was lean and reddish Steerpike!Squirrel doing all this time? Well, he was dancing attendance on Neo whenever the posse was around, and getting as close to the king as possible. Which meant he got jumped more often than not. Oddly, he didn't seem to mind. In fact, he seemed almost to provoke the king into a rage, by dancing about and chittering, full of high spirits and cheer.

Neo, doughty warrior that he was, lasted about a week.

A bright afternoon came, one of the hot ones we had months ago. The air was so wet it felt like breathing through a towel. The weather would whipsaw back and forth, one day raining, the next steam-jungle-hot enough to drive you to drink, and then make you sorry you'd taken down anything but water. It was wet and miserable, and even Miss B, the most cheerful dog on earth, had her snappish moments. Getting her to go outside to pee was a chore. "ARE YOU KIDDING?" she would mutter, looking sidelong at me. "HAVE YOU **BEEN** OUT THERE? IT'S DISGUSTING, AND I'M WEARING A FUR COAT."

And my soft but inflexible reply, "So help me, I am not having you pee on the rug. COME ON."

So out we went. I leaned against the house, watching as Miss B slunk about in the shade, searching for The Perfect Spot. Now, I want you to remember that she's lurking. Don't forget that.

Juliet!Jay and Romeo!Jay were in the pussywillow tree, canoodling softly. Mourning doves were in the neighbor's pines, exchanging comments on the weather and the old-man-pee smell of simmering juniper. Miss B slid around one corner of the house, seeking more shade.

Forth from the back corner, where the Headless Squirrel lay interred, came the posse, snapping their fingers[47]. Neo was at their head, and he had relaxed slightly. Steerpike was capering alongside, and Neo kept giving him sidelong little glances.

Suspicious glances.

I wished I knew how to speak squirrelese. "That's right," I breathed. "Suspect him. Oh, suspect him."

Steerpike kept capering. They moved out into the middle of the yard, tails twitching and noses lifted. I daresay there was even some sauntering going on. Steerpike, getting no reaction from Neo, turned his attention to a squirrel girl—oh, let's call her Bettina—and they gamboled rather acrobatically. Bettina!Squirrel used to be Neo's girl, but she had taken to avoiding him and hanging at the back of the posse. I didn't blame her. He'd jumped her once, and only Steerpike's intervention had avoided Severe Unpleasantness.

Because no matter how badly Neo's being gaslighted, I won't have squirrel domestic violence in my yard. That's why the Sekrit Weapon was near the sunroom door. Remember that, too.

The stage was set. I was a little uneasy, and I was watching Steerpike. Who was unconcerned, smiling and handsome, rolling in the sun with Bettina!Squirrel.

And then. Yes, you knew there had to be an "and then."

---

[47] West Side Story – Prologue
http://www.youtube.com/watch?v=bxoC5Oyf_ss

We heard him before we saw him. Mercutio!Jay coasted in, tail fluttering, in fine feathered form, landing on the ground near a bank of lemon balm[48]. "ON TOP OF OLD SMOOOOOOKEY, ALL COVERED WITH BIRDSEED—HEY EVERYONE! WHAT'S—AUUUGHTFUCKADOODLE! JESUS CHRIST!"

It was the final straw. Neo's nerves snapped. There was only a gray blur.

Mercutio went into the bank of lemon balm, screeching bloody murder. Feathers flew. "FIRE! MURDER! THIEVES! SMOOOOOOG[49]!"

Juliet!Jay hopped down, peering curiously into the green bank. I opened my mouth to protest, but she was already yelling. "WHAT THE HELL ARE YOU—ULP!"

Neo barreled out of the bank and hit her dead center.

And Romeo!Jay...well, he'd had *enough*, at that point. Nobody messes with Juliet while he's around. A streak of blue-feathered brilliance screaming "BAAAAAN-ZZZZAAAAAAI!" smashed into Neo, who was giving as good as he got. Rarely has there been such a display of kung-fu prowess in the Kingdom of Backyard.

You have to realize, this happened all within a few seconds. I was still inhaling to warn Julie when Miss B—remember her?—burst around the corner of the house, drawn by the ruckus. Every circuit in her little doggy brain fused. "HEEEEEEEERD IT!" she bellowed, and bolted across the yard.

All at once: Mercutio: "JESUS CHRIST!" Juliet: "AUGH!" Romeo: "JUUUUUULIE!" Neo was making THAT SOUND. Again. He was holding off three jays at once, including a maddened Romeo who didn't give a shit

---

[48] http://en.wikipedia.org/wiki/Melissa_officinalis
[49] http://blip.tv/toonjet-cartoon-channel/looney-tunes-what-s-opera-doc-911868

about kung fu, he was going to get his hammer and beat some ass[50].

Now, I am possessed of no sense at all. Instead of going to get my Sekrit Weapon, I took off barefoot across the yard, my own "OH FOR CHRISSAKE CUT IT OUT!" drowned in the hubbub. The combatants, at that precise moment, noticed the impending canine tornado.

"HEEEEEERD IT!" Miss B bellowed again, and the yard exploded.

You know how in cartoons there will be a stampede, dust flying and the camera shaking, and Bugs Bunny in the middle with his shoulders hunched, his ears flapping a little bit as everyone pours past him? Yeah. That was me. Squirrels at my ankles, the jays suddenly remembering they could fly, and Miss B streaking by so fast the wind of her passing hit my shins. Neo, cut off from the juniper hedge, crazed and screaming, bolted for the gate on the far side of the garage. Steerpike lolloped afterward, high-pitched terrifying laughter bursting out of him and adding to the chaos, Bettina and the others had nipped through the fence for the safety of the neighbor's pine trees, where the mourning doves were watching with bated breath and a great deal of interest.

Neo nipped between the gate and the garage wall. Steerpike ducked after him, still grinning. Miss B dug in, but was going too fast. She hit the gate with a yelp and a crash, backed up shaking her head, and turned in a circle a couple times, yapping with sheer joy and frustrated herding instinct.

Feathers drifted down. My ribs heaved even though I was standing still. I heard a deathly screech from the front yard.

This is not going to end well.

---

[50]Oldboy – Epic Fight
http://www.youtube.com/watch?v=Ufss5ot_vGE

I ran for the back door, wrenched it open, scooped up my Sekrit Weapon, and booked through my house for the front door, leaving Miss B to sort herself out.

You see, like Romeo!Jay, I'd had bloody well *enough*.

...to be continued.

SQUiRREL SHOWDOWN WEATHER

September 21ˢᵗ, 2011

S o there I was, in my driveway, waving a golf club and staring in openmouthed wonder.

When last we saw Squirrel!Neo, he had streaked between the fence and the garage after his little, um, psychotic break and the melee that followed. Behind him capered Steerpike!Squirrel, whose dastardly plan's culmination had exceeded his wildest hopes. Miss B was shaking off her concussion, the jays were screaming, and the rest of the squirrels had taken refuge in my neighbor's tall pine trees among the mourning doves[51], who immediately started gossiping softly about this turn of events. Worse than old ladies at a back fence, those doves. ANYWAY.

The day was still hot and sticky. Faraway thunder rumbled. Dark, stacked clouds were massing, but not nearly quickly enough. It was the kind of afternoon where people get drunk and angry, where it shades into an evening of more of the same and a night full of screams and punches.

---

[51] http://en.wikipedia.org/wiki/Mourning_Dove

In other words, it was showdown weather.

I managed to run through the house without tripping on anything, hit myself on the shins with my Sekrit Weapon, cleared the pet gate with a leap I am *still* proud of, whacked myself on the shins *again*, ran into my front door, twisted the knob, ran into it again (this was not my finest moment), finally figured out how to work my own goddamn door, piled out onto my front walk, and skidded to a stop.

Apparently I'd missed something while I was clocking myself on the head with my own front door; Neo had put two and two together and come up with Steerpike.

"YOU!" Squirrel!Neo bellowed. He'd lost a chunk of fur over his right shoulder, and blood striped his muzzle. But his crooked tail was high. "TRAITOR! THIEF! MONGREL! IMMA BEAT YO ASS!"

Steerpike!Squirrel grinned, panting. "BRING IT, OLD MAN. THERE'S A NEW KING IN TOWN."

Well, those were fightin' words. The duelists closed in a flurry of teeth and claws, and I was wondering if they both had rabies. I also had figured out I was barefoot, since I'd just been standing watching Miss B do her business. I also realized I was brandishing the Sekrit Weapon, and lowered the golf club somewhat sheepishly. I would have liked to wade in and give Steerpike a solid thump to his little rodent skull, but the chance of hitting Neo was too great. Plus, they were rolling all over my driveway.

Neo: THAT SOUND

Steerpike: "HAHAHAHA, YOU CAN'T CATCH ME, YOU CAN'T—" *Bam.* "DIDN'T HURT! YOU'RE TOO WEAK!"

Neo: THAT SOUND

Steerpike: "AND I'M GONNA LIKE BEING BETTINA'S SQUIRRELMAN, YOU KNOW." *Whap. Thud. Tearing noise.*

Neo: Silence.

The sudden quiet was eerie. Steerpike's only hope was his agility, and he kept dancing out of reach, darting in to smack or claw at Neo, who was like a damaged engine—terrible, but slow. Barking and crashing from the house behind me; Miss B had gotten over her head trauma, I guess, and found her way inside. I should have been hoping the pet gate would still be a deterrent. I should have been thinking about going back to close the front door, which was no doubt letting in a bunch of sticky air and nasty bugs. I should have been going to get the hose to separate the combatants—hey, it works for dogs, right?

Instead, I just stood, and stared, my shins throbbing. The incipient thunderstorm crept in front of the sun, eerie yellow-green stormlight filling every crack and crevice with odd shadows. Steerpike twisted, meaning to hop away. I don't know what he had planned, but it failed, because Neo jerk-twisted...and caught him.

In fact, Neo hit him so hard I heard the crunch at the top of the driveway, and they rolled out into the road.

In the distance, under a mutter of thunder, an engine growled.

...to be continued.

JACKASS!REDTRUCK AND THE SQUIRREL SHOWDOWN

September 23rd, 2011

The Old Squirrel King and the Traitor rolled out into the road. Thunder muttered, and an engine revved.

To explain this, I should tell you that people tear down our quiet little street all the time. You see, our street—all two and a half blocks of it—runs parallel to the main road coming into the neighborhood, but the main road has speed bumps. So, various idiots (usually angry soccer mums in minivans or overcompensating jackwads in BEEEG trucks) turn off the main road, turn onto our street, rev up to about forty miles per, just get up to speed when they have to brake and turn again...and stop at the stop sign, where they turn back onto the main road. It doesn't save them any time, nor does it help them get where they're going. I suppose they just feel like they've gotten one over on the Man, or something. Who knows? Some poor soul—probably a kid—is going to get run over one of these days, and maybe the city will put speed bumps in on our street too[52].

Anyway. Bleeding and battered and slowing down—for he was no spring chicken in squirrel years, our Neo, and he had already held off three jays and a crazed herding dog—the Old King had the Traitor flat on the pavement, and was beating the living hell out of him. "THROW SHIT AT **ME**, WILL YOU? TRY IT NOW! TRY IT **NOW**! **I KNOW KUUUUUUNG FUUUUUU!**"

And Steerpike!Squirrel, still laughing that crazy high-pitched maniacal laughter, had lost all his discretion. "I'M GONNA HAVE BETTINA, AND THE BACKYARD TOO! HAHAHAHAHA!"

Then there was Yours Truly, standing there barefoot with a golf club and an open mouth, the yellow-green bruise-light of an approaching storm falling over the entire scene with heavy sticky oppressive heat. Sweat trickled down my back, and the bright idea—*I could get the hose to calm them both down, I guess, that's what you're supposed to do for dogs, right?*—had just wandered through my stunned brain. (Look, I had just hit myself on the head with my own door, all right? YOU try thinking clearly in This Sort Of Situation, goddammit. I dare you.)

The engine growl became a screech, and it barreled past in a streak of candy-apple red. It was the jerkass in the red truck—every afternoon, bass thumping and meaty arm hanging out the window, this balding asshole races down our street. He doesn't content himself with going forty, like all the other jerkholes who zoom past. No, this former football star (you can just TELL he had his glory days in high school and hasn't forgotten them, you know the type) guns it around the corner, almost swiping

---

[52] We've since moved, but I hear from friends on our former street that this is still the case. *Plus ce change*, and all that.

whoever's waiting to turn left to get to the grocery (yes, that was me more than once) and floors it, trying to achieve sixty before he has to snap on his brakes. I don't know how many tons his truck is (it's got to be at least half to haul his huge ass around) but I know he probably has an itty-bitty wiener he is very sensitive about.

Like I said, you can just *tell*. ANYWAY.

I actually screamed. Yes, my chickadees, I let forth a Vader "NOOOOOOOO!"[53] I don't remember moving, but I was at the end of my driveway, pavement burning my feet, the golf club suddenly raised. Jackass Redtruck (for such I have dubbed him, and such will be the name called at the trump of Judgment when he is cast unto a fiery pit, and not a moment too soon please God) smashed his brakes. There was an unearthly screech—did I mention he has this truck that looks really shiny, but obviously he doesn't take care of it?—and smear-scream of rubber laid down.

I would like you, dear Reader, to imagine this. One wild-haired, sweating writer in jeans and a M*A*S*H T-shirt, waving a golf club, running down the street as a spear of lightning flashes, drenching the road with unholy white brilliance. Jackass Redtruck has his door half open and half his copious acres of ass out; I don't know if he was stopping to scoop up whatever had been in his way so he could take it home and stuff it[54], or what.

Thunder crackled. I realized what I was screaming. At the top of my lungs. As I ran down the road. With the golf club.

"YOU SONOFABITCH, YOU KILLED MY SQUUUUUUIRREL!"

---

[53] http://noooooooooooooooo.com/
[54] Official Ojai Valley Taxidermy TV Commercial
http://www.youtube.com/watch?v=LJP1DphOWPs

I think I saw him mouth one wondering "Holy *shit!*" before Jackass Redtruck piled back in, slammed the door, and gunned his engine. He raced around the corner and was gone, leaving me to put my own brakes on and stop, sides heaving and feet burning afresh, shaking the club as the rain began pattering down in quarter-sized drops.

Still screaming.

"THAT WAS NEO, YOU SONOFAHONKEY-TONK WHOREMONGERING BASTARD! **YOU KILLED MY SQUUUUUIIRREL!**"

Thunder rattled again. There was another flash of lightning in the distance. *Well, great,* I thought. *Oh, great. Dead squirrels and my God, the neighbors probably knew I was crazy, but this is just too much. Why me? Why can't I have normal wildlife around my house? Jesus.*

Then I realized something.

I hadn't actually seen Jackass Redtruck *hit* them, and the truck was jacked up pretty high. Maybe, just maybe...

I turned, very slowly, and looked down my street. And I saw...

...to be continued.

117

A GRAVE AND A BED

September 27th, 2011

The combatants lay on the road under a curtain of rain. Lightning flashed again. The water coming from the sky was blood-warm, each quarter-sized drop sending up a puff of dust where it hit the tired, dry ground, a sheen of dust and oil soon floating on a thin scrim of rain.

When we left off, Jerkass Redtruck had decided cowardice was the better part of valor and peeled away from the scene of the crime. Miss B was still crashing around and barking hysterically, apparently having worked off her concussion. My M*A*S*H T-shirt was soon sticking to me, and my bare feet were soaked by the time I reached the road at the bottom of my driveway. I was still clutching the Sekrit Weapon, and my hair was starting to drip in my face. Holding my breath, I approached the two sodden lumps of fur.

Blinking furiously, I could not figure out why my eyes were burning. There was another photoflash of lightning, and I saw what was what.

It wasn't pretty.

He lay on his back, guts actually spilling out of his exploded belly and his face turned up to the rain. His claws were outstretched, and already—how do they do it so soon?—a fly had found him. Thunder rattled, and even Yours Truly felt a little queasy. It's not every day I get so close to roadkill.

I held my breath, and looked at the other squirrel.

He appeared whole. His paws twitched a little. Maybe he was just dazed. I stood there for a second, in the rain, with the golf club, and thought it over. The rain intensified, and thunder boomed again. The law of first responding is to care for the living, right?

Inside the house, the thunder was muted but the rattling of rain on the roof was loud. Miss B was hysterical. "WHAT'S GOING ON? YOU'RE ALL WET! YOU SMELL WEIRD! WHAT HAPPENED? MY HEAD HURTS! WHEN'S DINNER? DO I GET A TREAT?" I got the front door closed and leaned against it for a second, then slowly put the golf club away. I petted Miss B absently on my way to the garage. The sound of the big garage door opening was lost in the rain, and a burst of fresh-washed wind tiptoed around my car. Miss B, left inside, scratched at the door, but I did *not* want her getting a snootful of dead squirrel. I spent about thirty seconds getting everything set up, then I turned toward the back corner.

It was time for the Shovel.

Now, as I've explained, the Shovel is a serious piece of work. It's flat, and red, and heavy—ideal for home defense. It was kind of ironic that now, when everything was said and done, I was better-armed. I trudged down my driveway and stood looking at the mess in the road.

"Shit," I muttered, and set to work.

Getting the dazed squirrel onto the shovel was kind of nerve-wracking. I mean, I expected him to shake off his torpor at any moment and decide I was a threat. He was heavier than you'd think—I flinched as he twitched again. Up the driveway and into the garage, where the sudden cessation of rain didn't wake him up either. His eyelids flickered and his wet furry sides heaved.

I settled him in the cat carrier, on top of the torn towel I was gonna get rid of anyway. I crouched there, the Shovel still at hand, and peered into the depths of the carrier. "I don't like you," I said quietly. "I've never liked you. But I am going to trust you not to destroy my goddamn garage while I get his grave done up. Then we'll talk."

Out into the rain again. My shirt was sticking to me like I was going to win a contest, my hair plastered to my head, and the thunder was getting closer. *It would just cap the whole goddamn thing if I got hit by lightning while burying a goddamn rodent*, I thought, and picked up the pace a little. The squashed squirrel wasn't looking any better, but I got most of him scraped up into the shovel. He was heavier than you'd think too, deadweight for real. Along the side of the house to the back gate, my face squinched up and dead squirrel held in front of me, I got the gate open and got through, closed it behind me. I headed for the back corner and the Headless Squirrel's grave.

Now, there was a dilemma. I didn't want squirrel guts getting all over everything while I dug the grave for the bits that remained. (Get it? Remaining remains? I kill me. Uh. Yeah.) Fortunately, I had Planned Ahead, and brought a big black rubbish bag. I got the remains unloaded onto it and began digging.

And then, I realized that in all the excitement, I'd forgotten to close the back door.

Miss B had her nose in the squirrel.

"JESUS CHRIST, THAT'S DEAD, LEAVE IT ALONE!" I screamed, and she jumped, guiltily. I weighed the likelihood of getting her inside, tried to catch her collar, and found out she thought this was some sort of game. "Oh, for *fucksake*, this couldn't be EASY, could it! Fine! Just stay out of the guts, okay?"

She was really interested, but she decided the corpse belonged to the alpha, so she'd wait for her bits like a good submissive pack member. I got the shovel worked into the dirt and began digging my second squirrel grave.

In the rain.

Again.

"DIGGING?" Miss B was beside herself. "OH PLEASE OH PLEASE, ME TOO! ME TOO!"

I'll gloss over that part. Suffice to say it was interesting, and I used language that would have scorched the ears off my sainted grandmother if she was still alive to hear me.

When it was deep enough to suit, I folded up the wet rubbish bag, and interred him with as much care as I could muster. Miss B had finally given up and cavorted in the rain, unable to understand what I was doing but distracted by WATER! OMG! FROMTHESKY! I filled in the grave, but there were no words of farewell. It was just raining too damn hard, and the flashes of lightning were getting closer together. I tamped the grave down, hoped it would be deep enough to keep Miss B out, and flat-out dragged my dog and the Shovel inside. The Shovel went in the sunroom, because dammit, I was going to dry off before dealing with this any further.

So it was that ten minutes later, I was sitting grimly at my kitchen table, shelling peanuts. (The Princess likes them, okay? There's no other use for them. NONE. I SWEAR.) I got a good bowl of them together and a bowl of water too while Miss B pounced on her rawhide in the living room, teaching it a lesson. "MY HEAD HURTS," she would remark occasionally. "TREAT? TREAT? FOOD FOR THE DOG?"

She'd already forgotten the excitement. A Zen creature of the Now, that's my Aussie. She didn't even protest when I gave her a sharp "No!" as she tried to follow me into the garage.

The driveway was a river. The rain came down in rippling sheets and lightning crashed, followed a bare two seconds later by thunder. I was a little more sanguine about my chances now, though.

I half expected the cat carrier to be empty. Apparently he had some sense, though, because when I cautiously crouched and peered in there he was. He'd moved, curling up in the back as far away from the wire door as he could get. I saw the gleam of one beady eye.

So he's still kind of ambulatory. Okay.

"You'd better not have rabies," I breathed, and very slowly, very gently, slid the bowl of water in. The bowl of peanuts was next, and I closed the door as quietly as I could. The spring locks made more noise than I liked, but I wasn't taking any chances. Then I sat back on my heels and realized what I'd just done.

"Don't get too comfortable. I'll check on you, and as soon as you're dead or recovered you're out of here. This doesn't mean I like you, and it doesn't mean we're friends. It just means I didn't leave you in the goddamn road."

I waited, but he said nothing. I hauled myself up and went inside, closing the garage door...

...leaving Squirrel!Neo alone to convalesce.

When he got better, things got interesting.

THE CONVALESCENCE OF NEO

October 13ᵗʰ, 2011

It was one of the few times in my life when I wished I played some form of incredibly violent team sport. Not only could I have used, say, hockey armor or an American-football helmet, but I also could have used some backup.

After all, I was going into the garage.

When last we left him, Squirrel!Neo, stunned and possibly concussed (that's a word, right?), was curled in a cat carrier in my garage. He had a bowl of shelled peanuts, a bowl of fresh water, and I'd made sure the cage door was locked. I spent a restless night, hoping I wouldn't have to dispose of yet another rodent corpse come dawn. I was running out of room in the Squirrel!Semetery. Though I wouldn't put it past another one of the little bastards to rise from the grave again.

So, the following fresh warm morning, I got up, nervously checked out the websites of a few sporting goods stores, and thought of dealing with the questions I would encounter if I went in and bought a whole set of hockey pads, helmet, greaves, the works. Kevlar seemed like a good option. Plus, a few hockey sticks would be a good addition to my Sekrit Weapon cache. Bonus if I could roll them in tar and ground glass.

Look, I was just being *careful*, okay?

In the end, I decided that one wounded squirrel in a cat carrier was probably not going to require me dressing up like a modern-day secutor[55]. I mean, Neo was probably feeling a bit under the weather, although I doubted even at that moment that he would be harboring so much as a tiny shred of gratitude toward the big pink monkey who had gotten him out of the road and shelled his fucking peanuts. *Probably*, I thought, *he's sleeping*.

That was my first mistake.

My car was in the garage, so I decided swinging a Sekrit Weapon around was not going to end well for anyone. Thus it was, that unarmed and foolish, I went where angels fear to tread. Miss B was clipped to the couch—no, I didn't staple her or anything. I just put her on a leash that has the other end below one of the couch legs. It's what we use to keep her from bolting over the pet fence and out the front door to catch, say, a tender, juicy UPS driver. Or a departing guest she likes too much to let leave. (Annie Wilkes[56] has NOTHING on Miss B, let me tell you.)

Yeah, well, we're working on Miss B's impulse control. She's getting better[57].

At least I had the presence of mind to put her on the leash, give her a Dingo bone[58] (there is very little she won't do for squeezy cheez or a Dingo bone; I like Cheetos so I figure we're about even) and tell her to stay. She obeyed me for a full five seconds before going to the

---

[55] http://en.wikipedia.org/wiki/Secutor
[56] Misery http://www.imdb.com/title/tt0100157/
[57] Monty Python- Bring Out Your Dead
http://www.youtube.com/watch?v=grbSQ6O6kbs
[58] http://www.dingobrand.com/

very end of the leash and giving me the Puppy So Sad You're-Stepping-On-My-Tiny-Dreams Look.

I already felt like a jerk.

ANYWAY. So I bopped to the garage door, listened intently, and heard nothing. Which wasn't at all unusual. I figured that if Neo was afoot in my garage, there would be Noise Of An Incredible Nature. All seemed quiet. Peaceful, even.

I twisted the knob and sallied forth into my carhaven. I left the door open behind me. I had some hazy idea of always leaving myself one avenue of escape. (It works out well in other areas of my life, okay? DON'T JUDGE.) Around the end of the car, thankful that the windows were rolled up, because all I needed was a squirrel in my *car* while I was driving down the street. (Remind me to tell you about how I had to have my windshield replaced that one time.) I took a deep breath, looked down at the cat carrier...

...and froze.

The steel-grill door to the cat carrier hung ajar, its hinges squeaking just a tiny bit to add dramatic tension to the moment. You could almost hear the horror-movie music swell. The towels were shredded, the peanuts were gone, and the water had been violently upset.

I guess King Neo had recovered.

Now seriously, Friends and Neighbors, I want to ask you: How is it even goddamn *possible* for a squirrel to open a cat carrier door with a spring-lock FROM THE FUCKING INSIDE? HOW? Because I DO NOT KNOW. It is one of those grand life mysteries, like where the other half of a pair of socks goes or how wire hangers mate.

"*Madre de Dios*," I breathed. "Neo, goddammit—"

"BANZAI!" he screamed, leaping from a pile of boxed foreign editions. "I KNOW KUNG FUUU-UUUUU!"

125

I flinched and screamed like a little girl, falling back against the car and barking my hip a good one. The car rocked on its springs, but Neo wasn't aiming for me. He was aiming for the car's roof, and he streaked across it like he was on wheels. Another leap, of effortless flying authority, and he vaulted from the hood...and barreled in through the door.

The open door. The door I had left open.

Into my house.

Into my goddamn kitchen.

In the distance, the barking began.

...to be continued.

THE BATTLE OF PELENNOR SUNROOM

October 28th, 2011

S HIT!" I screamed, as I skidded around the corner into my kitchen from the garage. "NO NO NO! NOOOOO!"

The squirrel wasn't listening. The dog, attached to the couch, was barking hysterically.

When we last saw Neo, he had voiced his battle cry and flung himself into my unprotected house. This was a fine way for the goddamn rodent to repay me for not leaving him in the road to die. Gratitude may be a virtue, but I really am beginning to think it's one this little asshole doesn't possess.

Several thoughts flash through one's head when one has inadvertently let a demonic tree-rat into one's house. Let me see if I can list them in some kind of coherent order.

1. OH JESUS CHRIST SQUIRREL RABIES AUGH!!!

2. None of this would have happened if I'd left him outside like a less goddamn charitable person would have.

3. A FUCKING SQUIRREL IN MY HOUSE!

4. How am I going to clean this up? Will bleach get squirrel out of the linoleum?

5. AUGH! SQUIRREL! WILD ANIMAL CRAWLING WITH FILTHDISEASENASTY IN MY KITCHEN!

6. I am really questioning my own intelligence at this point.

7. HOW DID HE GET OUT OF THAT FUCKING CAT CARRIER?

8. Thank God the dog is tied up—wait.

9. AND MY DOG IS TIED UP AND CAN'T DEFEND HERSELF AUGH!

10. The cats! OMG the cats!

11. HE KICKED ONE CAT IN THE HEAD, WHAT IS HE GOING TO DO TO THE OTHERS?

You get the idea.

I found out I was carrying an axe handle, and put on the brakes in the middle of my kitchen, barely aware I was screaming obscenities—

What? The axe handle? They're cheap, they make good weapons, and you can prop them near doors. I like having reasonable weapons in each room, and something within arm's reach at any moment. I AM PARANOID, OKAY?

The axe handle had been right by the garage door. I'd picked it up by the wrong end, but it can still be a bludgeon. At least it wasn't the Sekrit Weapon. And I just couldn't *throw* it, because with my luck it would go straight through a window, and explaining that to anyone who came to fix it would just not...wait, where was I?

Oh yeah. Middle of the kitchen, jerked up short like a dog on a chain, the chunk of wood in my left hand dangling once my arm dropped. The obscenities cut off midstream, I choked on something that sounded suspiciously like "—damn hamsterfucking crazyass rodent!" and froze.

An uneasy silence fell.

The cats, you see, had come to investigate the ruckus. Sweet dumb Tuxedo Kitty, who had been kicked in the head by Neo lo these many ages ago, Lemur!Cat, and CrankyOldDuck!Cat—our oldest, he's cranky, and if you surprise him he actually quacks. Like a duck.

Look, all my animals are strange. I can't help myself, I pick up the rejects and the outcasts. This explains not only the Duck Cat, the Stupid Tuxedo, and Miss B, but also my dating life. ANYWAY.

CrankyOldDuck!Cat, his oddly-shaped ears flat against his head, crouched and examined this New Thing In The House. He regarded it exactly the way he regarded Miss B when I brought her home. "WHAT IS THIS THING?" he grumble-quacked. "IT LOOKS SNACK-SIZED. PROBABLY TOO MUCH TROUBLE, THOUGH. WHAT THE HELL HAVE YOU DONE NOW, MONKEY?"

Tuxedo Kitty, eyes wide and tail twitching, was near the dining-room table. "I THINK I REMEMBER YOU," he was saying. "I'M ALMOST SURE I DO. HANG ON."

Lemur!Cat, huge, long, and lean, with a face that looks like a tree lemur's (cat's eyes are HUGE, OMG) and all the mental horsepower of a fat wet rock, stood chewing air and regarding this intruder with a gleam in his eye I'd seen a few times before. It was the gleam I saw, accompanied by the throaty *pleaseohplease* noises he was making now, right before he launched himself at the sunroom window to try to get at the birds at the feeder hanging outside.

He still hasn't grasped the nature of the barrier that bonks him on the nose each time. (He had some problems growing up, okay?)

Lemur!Cat's haunches went up. He crouched, and Neo, his tail twitching, stood at the edge of the rug. I cleared my throat, nervously, and nobody moved.

"Okay," I said, quietly. "Let's just all calm down and think about—"

"I KNOW KUNG FUUUUUUUU!" Neo took the only route of escape left, through the almost-closed glass door into the sunroom. I leave it open a bit so the cats can get out to their kibble and litter boxes, but closed enough so Miss B can't get her fat ass through it. (She has a distressing fondness for Catbox Roca.) I bolted for the door, to shut it before the cats got through. If he was in the sunroom I could go out through the garage and open the outer sunroom door, and he could get out into his kingdom once again.

I'm pretty fast, especially when spurred by adrenaline. However, I am no match for three cats. Lemur!Cat had sprung, and Tuxedo!Kitty, not wanting to be left behind, took off after him like a rocket. CrankyOldDuck!Cat, dimly understanding everyone was running for the Room What's Got The Kibble, let out a yowl and sprang forth to get his fair share.

"CHRIST NO NOT THE PLANTS!" I yelled.

Right before I ran into the sunroom door. I'm just goddamn lucky the chunk of wood in my left fist didn't shatter some glass and add to the fun.

Cursing, rubbing my nose, I wrenched the sunroom door open.

My plan at that point was to get through into the sunroom, close the door behind me, and open up the door to the backyard, *then* figure out how to get the goddamn squirrel out. The cats would probably chase him into the wild green yonder, and once Neo had some room to maneuver, I was a bit more sanguine about the end of this little episode not involving bloodshed, broken glass, and yowling. It was the best I could come up with. It was even a cunning plan[59].

---

[59] http://en.wikiquote.org/wiki/Blackadder

Unfortunately, the goddamn animals had other ideas.

Neo leapt for the high ground—the picnic table where I keep the jungle of houseplants I am nursing to health, or someone moved and I can't just throw them away, or I found them shivering on a street corner and just had to take them in. (SHUT UP.) Lemur!Kitty was right behind him, and the desperate battle was accompanied by my despairing cry and CrankyOldDuck!Cat quacking "ALL YOU KIDS STAY AWAY FROM MAH KIBBLE!" and Tuxedo!Kitty's yelling "I REMEMBER! I REMEMBER! YOU KICKED ME IN THE HEAD!" And Neo making THAT SOUND again, in between war cries involving "GONDOR NEEDS NO KUNG FUUUUUU!" and "FIGHT YOU AAAAAAAALLLL!"

I was still kind-of-thinking at this point. I wrenched the door to the outdoors open, trying not to break it with the axe handle, heard a terracotta pot shatter, and realized far too late that the dog was too quiet and I'd left the *other* sunroom door open.

From the depths of the house came help unlooked-for.

"HEEEEEEEERD IT!" she bellowed. "MUSTER THE ROHIRRIM! CALL UP THE DEAD! HEEEEEEERD IT!" She hit the doorway in a flurry of fur and baying. "I AM NO MAN!"

The quiet I'd noticed earlier? That had been her worming out of her collar. When a dog is motivated, I guess, miracles happen.

Three things that were *not* miraculous happened at once.

"JESUS CHRIST[60]!" I yelled.

---

[60] Holy Grail – Killer Bunny
http://www.youtube.com/watch?v=XcxKIJTb3Hg

"THE DOG! THE DOG!" the cats screamed in unison.

And, of course, "KUNG FUUUUUUUU!" Neo.

I now pause to inform you that Aussies, champion herding dogs that they are, consider things like a heavy-duty picnic table that weighs far more than *I* do not as a "deterrent" to rounding up and herding three cats and a squirrel. Nope. No, definitely not a "deterrent." More like "enjoyable but not very complex challenge."

I could only stand still...and watch.

THE PYRRHIC VICTORY OF PELENNOR SUNROOM

December 21st, 2011

Why do these things always end up with me barefoot and screaming? It must be Fate or some shit. I have to tell you, though, it's been so long I think I don't remember what happened next.

HAHA JUST KIDDING. It's burned into my tiny monkey brain like the sight of Sean Connery in *Zardoz*[61]. Anyway. When last we saw Neo, the cats, and my champion herding Aussie, they were all in my sunroom. Neo had expressed his thankfulness for me saving his psychotic squirrel ass by screaming and invading my house, and the cats had taken a vote and decided that they were going to chase the little furry demon. To be fair, Tuxedo!Kitty wanted revenge for being kicked in the head, and Lemur!Cat just wanted to chase something small and snackable without a window in the way. CrankyOldDuck!Cat just wanted to be sure nobody was going to eat his share of the kibble. And *then*, Miss B had

---

[61] http://en.wikipedia.org/wiki/Zardoz

gotten loose, and every circuit inside her doggy skull just fused together when she saw an opportunity to *heeeeeerd* something.

Let's halt the action here for a second, just press the pause button, as it were, and see what everyone is doing.

See that little gray blur, vibrating in place even though we've hit pause? That's Neo. He seems to have bounced back wonderfully from being hit by a truck. His tail, however, is more crooked than ever, and perhaps it's that throwing off his balance, because he's just fallen off the sunroom table and is hanging in midair.

The cats are caught in various poses. Cranky-OldDuck!Cat is hunched there by the kibble, his eyes wide and his crumpled ears pinned back against his skull. He has just realized that there is chaos afoot, but as long as it doesn't come near his food bowl, he's content to simply be a spectator. Tuxedo!Kitty, that black-and-white streak there? He's hanging in midair too, spread out like a starfish and hissing, because he has just realized the noise means that the dog has joined in the fun. (More on the dog in a bit.) Tuxedo!Kitty, sweet and dumb and stupid as he is, has not adjusted well to Miss B's presence in our household. In fact, he actively plots her demise, but she thinks he's cute and fluffy. Which, of course, leads to Hijinks.

Anyway. Lemur!Cat, long and deceptively lean for such a big feline, has just hit the floor and is in the process of gathering himself to levitate again. (That DERP on his face isn't effort or the thrill of the chase, it's his natural expression. He had some...problems, growing up.)

And who is that on the table, big huge doggy grin spreading drool everywhere, caught in the act of knocking every blessed plant off and onto the concrete floor? The one who had just landed in the middle of the cat boxes, causing an explosion best left to the imagination and popping back up like a jack in the box, her battle cry ("GONNA STICK ME SOME NAZGUL, I AM NO MAAAAAAAAN!") rattling the sunroom's windows and doors?

Why, it's Miss B.

But wait.

Because she's not just there. She's also crouched in front of the sunroom steps, head down and snaking, ready to nip at Lemur!Cat's hindquarters to drive him toward the open door to the backyard. She is *also* on the treadmill, claws digging in as she tries to nose Squirrel!Neo out of the air and into the proper direction.

I believe I have found the source of her ability to herd. It lies in being in multiple places at once. Or maybe the pause button is defective, who knows?

Well, we've let them rest long enough. Let's hit play again.

CRASH. SHATTER. BANG. "Noooooooo! Not the plants!" My cry of despair. (I kind of understand how Faramir must have felt seeing his city get the crap beaten out of it.) "GOD DAMN YOU ALL!" Shaking the axe handle, and then, I realized...

...that I was right in the path of the hurricane, so to speak.

If you've never seen a forty-plus-pound dog on top of a picnic table, baying frantically as her claws dig in (there are gouges in the top of the table you would not *believe*) and launching herself like Supergirl, well, you've missed out. Her tongue was out, and she looked about as joyful as it's possible for a flying canine to look. She cleared the treadmill's arms and landed on the other side, on a long wooden bench that had been holding up yet more plants. I say "had been" because the sudden application of her force on one end had predictable results, and if I had not hit the deck I might have been brained by a flying philodendron. (It only missed the glass door by a miracle.)

A misspent youth in the middle of barfights is far from the worst training for this sort of thing. I'm just sayin'.

This left me on the floor, staring as a crooked-tailed squirrel landed, got his feet under him, screamed "GONDOR NEEDS NO KUNG FUUUUUUUU!" and bolted past me for the yard.

Lemur!Cat, committed to his leap, actually landed *on* me, and he was wearing his cleats for better traction. I screamed, sort-of-crawfishing on the floor as potting soil showered down on me, and smacked him. Even though the cat is a moron, he's still incredibly agile. He twisted in midair....and collided with the dog, who dropped straight down and nipped at Tuxedo!Kitty, who did not know whether to shit or go blind at this point. The sudden appearance of an OCSA (Object of Canine Size and Appearance) was too much for him, and he bolted out into the yard. Lemur!Cat, landing on the treadmill, gave another sideways leap, but Miss B actually caught him with her nose again and heaved him, neatest trick of the week, out the door.

Then she leapt over me, paws outstretched. "FUUUUUUN!" she barked. "RIDERS OF ROHAN, TO ME, TO ME!" She landed in an explosion of bark mulch outside the open door, and I found myself bleeding and barefoot, lying on the concrete floor and clutching an axe handle, in a suddenly echoingly-empty sunroom.

Well, kind of empty. CrankyOldDuck!Cat still crouched by his food bowl. "THAT WAS AMAZING," he quacked. "I'M HUNGRY."

I scrambled, aiming to get to my feet but only making it to hands and knees. Somehow spilled out the door and got my legs underneath me—look, I was not the

136

picture of grace, but you wouldn't be either if you'd just been beaten by a cat the size of a fat raccoon with the mental horsepower of a damp brick—and halted at the edge of the pavers I'd put down so I didn't have to stand in the mud while Miss B did her business out in the yard. The stone was cold, the shirt I was wearing was never going to be the same, and I realized I was calling down curses on every animal in a fifty-mile radius at the top of my lungs.

I told you, these things *always* end up that way.

Out in the yard, grass flying and tongue lolling, my dog had two cats and a crazed squirrel bunched up, and she was trying to herd them. Despite a stunning display of athletic prowess and outright bi-(or tri-)location, such a feat was beyond her skill.

Still, she gave it a good go. The battle ended with Neo nipping under the juniper hedge still screaming about how Gondor knew kung-fu, and the cats scattering like marbles dropped on the kitchen floor. Lemur!Cat squeezed under the fence near the plum tree, leaving some fur behind in the process, and Tuxedo!Kitty just barely made it to the side of the garage and through a gap there. Miss B pulled up short, saving herself just barely from crashing into the gate on the garage side of the house, shook her fur, and looked over her shoulder at her human, who was still shaking the axe handle and yelling.

"...sonofa*bitch*," I finished lamely, and had to stop for breath. I wiped potting soil off my forehead with a damp hand—look, I was sweating, you would be too—and whooped in a deep inhale. Miss B trotted to me, her skirts switching.

"THAT WAS FUN," she announced. "MORE? THROW A BALL? PLAY? FOOD? TIME FOR FOOD?"

It was at that moment I decided that never again would I feel charitable toward a tree-rodent. It took me two days to clean up the sunroom, and one of the jade plants never recovered from the shock. (It's still shuddering and whispering "—*and then I fell, and then I fell...*" over and over again.) It took a week and a half for the claw-marks in my side to heal, and Lemur!Cat had to be coaxed back inside with tuna fish. Tuxedo!Kitty spent the night in parts unknown, and showed up the next morning loudly bitching at the dog and actually hissing at me for good measure.

I kept a sharp eye out for the goddamn kung-fu squirrel, but I guess he had to hole up somewhere and recover from his convalescence. It was a damn good thing, too, because the next time I saw him he had an angry girlfriend punching him in the face. I guess the King of the Backyard never gets a break...

...but that's another story.

AFTERWORD

I always intended to write more Squirrel!Terror. Sadly, Tuxedo!Kitty and CrankyDuck!Cat fell ill—neither were spring chickens—after Lemur!Cat disappeared one night. There was also the little matter of buying a house and moving. After losing three cats, cranky and terrible as they were...I just couldn't write more about Neo, although I could tell how he lost his eye to his love Bettina, and was still ruling the backyard as a warrior king when we left. I could tell about the Bartholomew vs Mercutio duel, and about how Lemur!Cat solved a mystery of a headless robin, and many other things. Every time I try to, though, I think of my poor cats. And I just can't.

Sometimes I drive past the old place, and I wonder if Neo's still around. Of course Bartholomew found me, and often I think I hear Mercutio yelling about iambic pentameter. When Neo eventually falls, as a squirrel inevitably does, I hope some kind soul buries him decently, or that by some adventure he receives a warrior's cremation.

Of course, I wouldn't put it past the little bastard to reincarnate, just so he could terrify my backyard once more.

The new place is nice. I like it. There are critters here too—Napoleon!Squirrel, his nemesis the Squirrelproof 5000 Deathride and his love Josephine, the Gentlecritter Masques and their cousin Cletus, the Hummingbird Twins and our sweet little bulldog puppy, Odd Trundles, who joined us due to a long chain of misadventure and luck both good and bad. I've started chronicling the new *backyard, in dribs and drabs. Maybe I'll make a book out of that too.*

I'm often told by other people that their backyards aren't nearly as interesting. I invite you, should you think so, to look closer, and look again. Chances are you'll find hilarity and tragedy in equal measure, in the creatures that share our spaces. You may even see a squirrel with a crooked tail and a glint of hellfire in his gaze, resurrected or reincarnated and ready for more. If you do, congratulations, and my condolences.

Oh, and, if you do see him...

...tell him I said hello.

ABOUT THE AUTHOR

Lili lives in Vancouver, Washington, with two dogs, two guinea pigs, two cats, two children, and a metric ton of books holding her house together. However, referring to her as "Noah" will likely get you a lecture.

ALSO BY LILITH SAINTCROW